THE GREEN FIE

Recent Titles from Evelyn Hart

MOUNTAINS OF THE SUN
SPRING IMPERIAL
THE STARS STILL SHINE

THE GREEN FIELDS BEYOND

Evelyn Hart

Evelyn Hart

SEVERN **SH** HOUSE

This first world edition published in Great Britain 1995 by
SEVERN HOUSE PUBLISHERS LTD of
9–15 High Street, Sutton, Surrey SM1 1DF.
First published in the USA 1995 by
SEVERN HOUSE PUBLISHERS INC of
595 Madison Avenue, New York, NY 10022.

British Library Cataloguing in Publication Data
Hart, Evelyn
    The Green Fields Beyond
    I. Title
    823.914 [F]

    ISBN 0-7278-4823-2

Typeset by Hewer Text Composition Services, Edinburgh.
Printed and bound in Great Britain by
Hartnolls Ltd, Bodmin, Cornwall.

To the memory of Jim who so gallantly wore the black beret.

"Through *mud* and *blood* to the *green* fields beyond."

Royal Tank Regiment colours
of brown, red and green.
"Fear Naught"
RTR motto

Part One

Chapter One

I saw him for the first time at a Sandhurst Ball. The year was 1935 and the event was drawing to its close. My partner, John Shawe, who had invited me after meeting me only briefly at my friend Dulcie's house, was of good height, but this man was much taller. Powerfully built, his fine figure immaculately clad in dress blues, he stood out head and shoulders above the others.

What is this phenomenon that draws total strangers to one another at a glance? I looked up, pulled by some sixth sense by his steady gaze across the crowded and noisy dance floor. Through the blare of the jazz band and the high decibles of excited young people, our eyes met in a moment of suspended time. For a second it was as if no one else but us two were in the room. Then John swept me off in a quick step.

I saw him again, this time dancing and searching over his partner's head. I knew that he was looking for me, only me, and a feeling of sublime ecstasy filled my body from head to toe.

A 'Paul Jones' was announced. We girls made a circle while the men ringed around us. The tall man passed me and we smiled, an almost intimate smile, at one another. By the time the music stopped again he had manoeuvred himself near. He grabbed me, pushing lesser mortals away, and I found myself dancing with him.

"Phew!" he said with a grin. "That was tricky."

I was quite unable to speak. I was overwhelmed at being in the arms of this giant, my head coming up to his shoulder. This stranger must have been six foot six in his socks – a gift to a tall girl like me. A gift? I did not think I had a hope with such a specimen, though my aunt had told me I was looking my best that night. She had persuaded me to go – I had not wanted to come. I had scarcely met John who had got the party together, and I did not know any of the others invited. But my aunt said Sandhurst Balls were 'quite something', and she was sure I would enjoy it. I would be fetched and returned by car with some other girls who lived in London. She said that I really must get over being so shy now that I was seventeen and had been 'finished' in Italy. So I went, and found I got on easily with John who seemed to like me and danced with me more than any of the other girls.

I was wearing my first ball dress, one in a soft salmon colour with yards of tulle which floated round my slim figure. On one thin shoulder strap was attached a spray of softly petalled artificial flowers over which I had sprinkled some Chanel No. 5 scent I had been given for Christmas, and I wore some rather sophisticated hooped earrings in gold to match the bracelet which had belonged to my mother.

"I spotted you across the room. I like tall girls. For me a small woman can be the very deuce to dance with," my partner smiled down at me. It was a rather whimsical smile that crinkled up the corners of his eyes and brought a dimple to his lower cheek. If I

4

had not already fallen in love with him, that smile would have done the trick.

"Yet look at all the tall men who marry small women. They say the opposites attract," I observed.

"Then not in this case, though we're opposites with me scowlingly dark and you angelically fair." He said it gently. Was he teasing? Was he a flirt?

"How long have you been here?" I asked quickly to hide the embarrassment I felt at his remark which I did not know how to take.

"The statutary two years. Just had our passing out parade. What a relief to have got through without being kicked out!"

"You've always wanted to go into the army?"

"Dead keen," he laughed. "My mother inspired me with her tales. She came from a line of distinguished generals."

"I hear the course is pretty gruelling," I remarked, thinking of how John had described it.

"Particularly to begin with. Inordinant amount of square bashing. One has to learn to take being screamed at by a sadistic sergeant-major. But one's got used to it from O.T.C. days at school; worth it for the impeccable turn-out we presented yesterday."

Instructions came over the loud speaker to return to circling for the "Paul Jones". "Let's get out of here," he expressed impatiently. He led me to a room where the remains of a large buffet was laid out.

"A drink?" he asked.

"No thank you," I declined. I was on lemonade and had already consumed sufficient quantities of it to drown me that evening. "It's late. What about you?"

"Same answer. I've been put in charge of my kid sister, so I'm on my best behaviour or my parents will

5

have something to say." He looked round for a place to sit. All seats were taken by chattering couples. "Better try below," he suggested.

I did not know what he meant by 'below' but I followed him blindly in my state of miasma. We went along a wide corridor flanked by pictures of old battle scenes, and down a dimly lit concrete staircase into what looked like a dungeon, or rather an arched crypt where I half expected to see tombs. For a moment I wondered if I was going to be violated, it was so dark down there, though I felt if it came to that it would not be quite so terrible to have it happen with this man. If it did happen, it would be my fault. How many times had my aunt warned me never to 'pick up' strange men?

"Breakfast. Like some?" Far from violating me he gestured to a series of loaded candlelit tables under further arches where chefs, in high cook's hats and white aprons were frying eggs and bacon, tomatoes, mushrooms, bread, sausages, kidneys – the whole gambit – on flaming oil stoves, and ladling the contents out onto plates for the consumption of the young.

"Not for me. I couldn't eat a thing. But don't let that spoil your appetite," I said politely.

"You're hopeless. You won't eat and you won't drink," he observed with amusement. He led me to a pillar near where other couples were sitting on trestle chairs, plates on laps. We sat down, stiffly facing one another.

"I shouldn't be here. My – my partner . . ." I stammered.

"Nor should I. My sister will be furious at my deserting her and the other girls."

"What girls?" I asked feeling intensely jealous.

"Friends of my sisters. You must meet her. She's not a bit stuffy."

"She probably wouldn't approve of me. I mean . . . I'm a pick up. Do you make a habit of picking up girls?"

"You're the first," his face crinkled. "I think I will go in for it; much more fun than sticking to one's party. We'd better introduce ourselves and make it proper! I'm Gough Nicholson, at your service ma'am," he smiled. The smile would have melted me if it had not done so already. "Your turn?"

"Isabelle de Montefort," I pronounced, and proceeded to apologize for it as I always did. The only time I felt I did not have to explain was on the Continent where it went down big. "My father came from Wicklow, Huguenot country. The Irish are very like the French in many ways."

"Isabelle," he repeated thoughtfully. "What a lovely name for the beautiful girl I spotted from across the room."

"If I am tonight, it is only because . . ." It was on the tip of my tongue to say "because of meeting you". I stopped myself just in time, and blushed to think I had nearly been so presumptuous. I hoped the cellar was dark enough to hide my blush.

He looked at me intently, and then said very seriously: "Strange things that usually only happen in novels are happening tonight. I would like to know where you live. I don't want to lose you the moment I've found you."

"London. And you?" Again, could he really mean it?

"Dorset; the family have been there since the Dark

7

Ages. My people also have a flat in London which my sister and I can use. I suppose you live with your parents, or are you a working girl?"

"I do work, but I live with a great-aunt." Oh dear, it was going to go wrong. Girls in his sort of set did not live incredibly dull lives with ancient aunts. "I'm an orphan," I said with truth, and at the same time hoping to make my circumstances sound more interesting. "My father was killed in the Great War in Mesopotamia, when I was only a few months old, and my mother, weakened by my birth in a difficult labour, and then grief at the loss of my father, died soon after in the influenza epidemic of 1919. I don't remember either of them."

Gough did not commiserate on this sad rigmarole, as most people did when told. Instead, all he said was, "Lucky great aunt." I could feel my face glowing at the implied compliment.

There was left a silence between us. Afterwards I thought of all the things that could have been said, things which needed badly to be said, during that pause. I gauged at the time that he did not like to intrude too much in asking questions. He was not a brash sort of person as some of my boy friends were who could jump in with both feet to annoy or mortify. I sensed that he was waiting for me to make the next move. What move? I could not give him a telephone number because we did not have a telephone, and I did not like to give the address of our dingy little flat at the top of a large house in Holland Park. I did not want this gorgeous man whose wealthy people lived in a country house in Dorset, and who had a posh flat in London, to meet my aunt who had become old and forgetful and was inclined to repeat herself

8

and drop her food. I went hot and cold all over at the mere thought. What would he think of us? It would ruin everything.

"I must go back," I rushed. "My partner will be wondering what has happened to me."

"Same here I suppose," he said reluctantly. He did not move.

"Come on then." I kicked myself the moment I had said the words. Idiot to have broken up our *tête à tête* sooner than I need and before we had established . . .

We climbed the stairs silently together, my heart sinking with every step at the thought of the imminent parting. I knew nothing about him. I had not even asked what regiment he was destined for.

At the entrance to the ballroom we bumped into John, looking distracted. "Oh, good, *there* you are," he expressed in relieved tones. "This is our dance. Where on earth have you been? I began to think I'd lost you."

You have, I thought, if you but knew it. Instead I said possessively as if I knew Gough well, "John this is Gough Nicholson. Gough, may I introduce John Shawe." The two cadets shook hands. Then Gough turned to me and we shook hands formally. His hand was strong and warm and altogether lovely in mine.

"We'll meet again," Gough said, deep-voiced. He looked at me very directly, one eyebrow raised.

When I thought about it afterwards I realized that this had been a question, an opening for me to give some way in which he could get in touch with me. But I was so inwardly flustered and overcome at the time, that, though I took in the words, the query in his voice went over my head.

9

"Let's get going or this dance will be over," John said, and he pulled me onto the floor. "Quite a man," he observed as we danced, the admiration showing in his voice. "Sort of natural leader and born soldier. I bet he goes far."

I nodded, too full of my own emotions to speak. So it was not only me who felt the man's magnetism. Men did too. As for nice John . . . when one meets the outstanding all other men seem small in comparison.

I was driven back to London with the other girls, and in the early hours I crept into the flat hoping not to disturb my aunt. There was little I could hide from her and I was relieved therefore when she did not call, but slept on. Once in my room I threw myself face down fully dressed upon my bed overcome by emotion, caring nought that my salmon pink dress lay in disorder about me, the artificial flowers crushed. I knew there would be no sleep for me during the few hours that were left of that night. I knew that my life would never be the same again.

So this was *love*, the phenomenon much talked about by the girls at the French Lycée in South Kensington where I had been educated (my Aunt was keen that I should become fluent in languages), a word I had giggled at and scarcely believed in. And it was every bit as wonderful, intense and total as the girls had said it was. But no one had told me it was also *hell*.

I lay on my bed gripped by an agony of despair with a hopeless love for a man I did not know and would in all probability never see again, for through my own shyness and John's having pulled me abruptly onto the dance floor, I had missed my opportunity.

I would not try and get in touch with Gough Nicholson myself even if I were able to. Convention, even as far on in the twentieth century as 1935, dictated that the male had to make the first move.

Fool that I was, I had thrown my chance of incredible happiness away.

John told me later that Gough in his last year at Sandhurst was a SUO – a Senior Under Officer – and although he had never met him, being in different Companies, he had watched him rowing for the Royal Military College at various aquatic events and had often noticed his exceptionally tall figure about the place. Was there a faint hope that a man of Gough's authority would not just sit back and do nothing about getting in touch with me? But how? Not through John, unless Gough too was destined for the Gunners. The chances that they might meet on the morning after the Ball when the Academy was breaking up for the summer vacation, were slender. Gough would most probably be going to his home in Dorset while John, I knew, was going to his in Suffolk. All would be packing cars and rushing to leave.

Doubts began to creep in. Gough may not *want* to seek me out; might not give me another thought. Yet I *had* attracted him in the f irst place, and I felt those exceptional looks displayed an open face too genuine for insincerity to be hidden behind that very direct deep brown gaze. The nose was Roman handsome, the lips full and curved . . . I could recall every inch of his features. I liked the fact that he did not wear

11

a moustache as most military men did. Those I found slightly comic whether of the large cavalry-type or the too-small ones which reminded me of Charlie Chaplin! I preferred a clean-shaven man after the photographs I had of my father, though I tolerated John's small rather youthfully sprouting one.

I went on castigating myself. Why had I become tongue-tied? Why had I interrupted our conversation so early on to say I must get back to my party? What would it have mattered if John *had* accused me of bad manners in leaving the gathering for another man? It was all my great aunt's fault. She had brought me up in the strict ethics of her generation as to what was done and what was not done, and one *did not abandon the person who paid for one's ticket*. In much the same way, if one received two invitations which clashed, one stuck to that which had come first and had been accepted, even if the second was to the most sought-after dinner and dance party in London. No excuses! There had been tears over such an event – to no avail.

It was also *Gough's* fault. Why had he not *demanded* an address? I assuredly would have given it. But then Gough would not demand. I could see that I had come up against an unusually discriminating character, one who may have been a born leader, but was also a sensitive man. Neither did I think he was the type who would chase girls. He was basically a man's man, as John had perceived. Exceptionally – most exceptionally – he had sought me out; he had said "I don't want to lose you", and later, the query, "We'll meet again?" I was a very lucky girl to get that far with such a man. That far and no further it seemed . . .

* * *

12

I did not tell my aunt about Gough, though I think she guessed from my moody silence after I had blurted out that I had met an "outstanding" man at the Ball. The next time I saw John, he rather surprisingly asked me if I was engaged to Gough Nicholson.

"What makes you think that?" I questioned, thinking if only it *were* true.

"You seemed, er, sort of familiar with one another . . . I mean you make quite a pair," John replied in his rather hesitant manner at anything personal.

"No, not engaged." I did not tell him that we had seen each other across the dance floor for the first time that evening and had spent a bare twenty minutes or so together before we parted to go back to our parties. Neither did I mention that I had had no communication with Gough since. As he seemed to think so, I let it stand that we were old friends. Later, much later, I asked John if he by any chance had heard more of the man I had introduced him to at the Ball. I had rather lost touch, I said in as offhand a manner as I could muster. No, John had not heard anything.

For me it became one of those once in a lifetime encounters as brief as brief but never ever forgotten.

Sadly, Gough Nicholson went completely out of my life without hardly ever having been in it.

As the days of heartbreak for a man I barely knew lengthened into weeks, months and then years, I lost hope of ever seeing Gough again. Even so I used to search the engagements Column in *The Times* in case his sister was to be married and there might be an indication of an address. I was not worried about Gough becoming engaged. I knew that a professional soldier such as he, starting out in his career at the age of nineteen or twenty was too young for that. I even used to run an eye over the deaths in case one of his parents passed on and I might find a clue to his whereabouts there. I must have wasted hours scanning engagements, marriages, and death columns.

Chapter Two

I may have lost hope of ever meeting Gough again, but I never forgot him. First love which can hit like a bolt from heaven and leave one bathed in dazzling sunlight, surely can never be forgotten. In my case I knew that though I might come to love other men, no man could ever in my estimation quite come up to Gough Nicholson.

In a way I resented Gough for having done this to me, for being so outstanding, for coming so strongly into my life and then, after the briefest of times, vanishing from it and taking with him those exquisite minutes of pure unadulterated joy which had given a new dimension to my whole existence. I might find happiness elsewhere, but never again would I experience such magic.

However, my encounter with Gough did not stop me from enjoying myself in a hurrying, busy, purposeful London; one that at night sparkled with theatres and dance clubs. By day the streets were packed with smartly dressed and hatted women descending in their furs from chauffeur driven cars to do their shopping in Knightsbridge or Bond Street. Their cars would go round and round the block and always seemed to turn up at the right place and right time to pick up their mistresses plus innumerable packages.

Even as an impecunious girl I had no need to carry a shopping basket. If one had no limousine, and could not afford a taxi, all would be delivered within the day to one's flat or house.

Having lived there nearly all my life, I was a true Londoner. I knew every inch of the West End and did not get lost even in a pea-souper when I could barely see a yard ahead. Then, above ground, transport was of no use. Even seasoned taxi men who had been born within the sound of Bow Bells could get disorientated. Everyone walked. On occasions I walked for miles to get home in a pea-souper. It was rather fun – a sort of adventurous emergency. Strangers greeted one another cheerily as they passed; groups stood under lamp lights trying to get their bearings, the puff of their breaths adding fog to the yellow glow.

I once, in the dim of a foggy night, met a man who stopped and asked me if I could help him. He was hopelessly lost!

"Where do you want to go to?" I asked.

"Notting Hill," he replied. As that was on my way, I told him to come with me. We kept on bumping into one another so I took his arm and we, complete strangers, walked companionably back, chatting away, to his doorstep where I left him. He was a young art dealer learning his trade at 'Spinks', and the next time I saw him he arrived in a taxi to take me out to dinner. We became great friends and some years later Denys asked me to marry him. His was a household name in the antique world, but by then . . . as shall be told . . .

I loved my London, loved leaping onto moving buses or going down into the blowy soot-smelling

16

depths of the warm, safe undergrounds, so much faster than on the surface where policemen held up the traffic for seemingly endless periods. Efficient though the London Bobbies were at directing the traffic, the method caused huge jams. Sometimes in the mornings it took me three-quarters of an hour to get to Bond Street from Holland Park by bus.

I always wore black when going out: black coat and skirt, little black hat perched on fair hair worn longish and turned under – all the rage. Black shoes, handbag and gloves were *de rigueur* for the West End. To relieve the black I, with most others, wore a softly-coloured blouse and sheer flesh-coloured silk stockings clocked over the ankles, the rib rolled up to lie absolutely straight at the back.

I knew many people in London: some from the City, bankers, lawyers, barristers, stockbrokers, Harley Street consultants' families. Some were in trade having started up shops of specialized luxury goods, and quite a few were in the musical world, and gave my aunt and myself tickets to concerts and the ballet and occasionally – an enormous treat – the opera.

After returning from that year in Italy, I had had more invitations than I could cope with. I had picked up with my old London school friends, and my friend Dulcie used our spare room, a tiny box-room under the eaves, as her *pied-à-terre* when in Town.

I was not in the society set who were presented at court, for to be in that one had to have money. In any case I thought it would be silly for me to try and keep up with the rich set of girls out to get titled husbands. Dulcie, whose parents *were* titled, agreed. *She* was

17

out to get an honours degree, and get it she did at Oxford – brilliantly.

I did not try to compete with her. "You are the one with brains," I used to say. "You are the one with the looks," she would reply. And we laughed. Dulcie was a dear: full of fun and sparkling with intelligence. Why she never seemed to have any suitors I could not imagine. Perhaps her intellect scared men off.

Anyway, I believe I can say without vanity – I was never self-assured enough for that – that I knew I looked good in my little black outfit, and this was borne out when I was asked to model for a small, select dress shop in Knightsbridge. This was no cat-stage walking to music, but simply a few twirls to show off the dresses and outfits chosen by wealthy customers from the garments put before them. Behind a curtain, I would quickly don the required dress, then come out and do my twirls, let the customer feel the material of the garment, then retreat and change into another. Easy! My friends thought it a 'glamorous' job. To me it was just fun putting on all those stunning outfits I could never afford. The hours in the salon were not long; it suited the times I was living in, and it augmented my pocket money.

I had no money of my own, but my Aunt Dora gave me as much as she could out of her small income from investments. Practically all my allowance was spent on clothes, plus tennis and skating – my two recreations. One could live and have a good time on very little in London then. Even the most impecunious of boyfriends would have been deeply offended had I produced a purse out of my bag and offered to help pay. I only went 'Dutch' with girlfriends.

Soon, John had become my "steady". He would come up from Woolwich to take me out; and in return I invited him to any formal invitation which had 'and partner' written on it. Funnily enough, even in London, there were never enough spare men, with the result that those there were much sought after. The nicest ones were always leaving to go out to India, Africa or to America to seek their fortunes.

So John was a boon, particularly as he never seemed short of money with which to take me out. I gathered a godfather had left him a lump sum – which he was rapidly blowing – and his parents were reasonably well-off. He would take me out to dinner at the Café Royal and on to a show after when we would dance until the small hours in the Four Hundred or some other favoured night-club. These were frequently raided by the police. No one seemed to take much notice, and they were always open again the next night.

John was the most undemanding of men. A few good-night kisses in the taxi on the way home after a late night was all that passed between us. I preferred it that way and he never pressed me for more. I suppose it was my total innocence that stopped even men with a reputation for getting off with girls from attempting to go further. I willingly gave of my lips for the good-night kiss that was expected at the end of an evening. Such a trusting kiss abashed many a man! One, an older bachelor who had a reputation for being something of a roué, after kissing me good-night on a doorstep, asked whether I 'felt anything'.

"Felt?" I said, big eyed. "What am I supposed to feel?"

With speed he backed away down the steps. He never asked me out again! Occasionally a married man appeared in our group, obviously in search of a girl with whom to have an affair. My responding kiss in a taxi or on a doorstep was enough to wing him on his way in search of lusher pastures!

I did, however, know one girl who for the rest of her life desperately regretted the situation she had got herself into. It never occurred to her to blame the man. She found out where she could have a backstreet abortion for which she paid the earth. She came out of it looking a pale wreck of the robust girl she had once been. Subsequently, when married, she discovered that the abortionist had made such a hack of it that she could not have children. She never regained her health. It ruined her life.

Definitely not for me. I would stick to my wholesome good-night kisses. Inevitably, I suppose, a man like John who was not yet in a position to marry, asked me to wait for him until he was 'on the strength' and would be entitled to a marriage allowance and married quarters. As he was then still only a lieutenant, that was going to take some time. I was flattered by my first offer of marriage, however remote in reality, but also glad that I did not have to answer 'yes' or 'no', but could reply unequivocally, "Let's wait and see when the time comes."

So time passed pleasantly and even happily, though always at the back of my mind there was the rememberance of Gough and the pang in my heart for him. In bed at nights I would lie awake wondering where he was and what being embraced by *him* would be like. And I would go over and over again every word that had passed between us in that desperately brief meeting.

Things began subtly to change in London. We had a new monarch: King Edward VIII. He was due to be crowned in May 1937 and for his coronation procession John booked seats at John Lewis' in Oxford Street.

"Terribly expensive," I gasped when he handed me my ten guinea ticket to keep until the day.

"We mightn't be alive to see another coronation, particularly if there is going to be a war," he remarked grimly. I heard the seriousness in his voice and for the first time felt a frisson of fear for what might come.

The abdication took us all by surprise. The press had kept an admirable silence about the King's paramour right from when he was Prince of Wales. All we knew of Mrs Ernest A. Simpson and her husband was from the court circular announcing that they had been invited to some 'do' at Buckingham Palace, or that they had arrived at Balmoral Castle for a visit. More usually it was to Fort Belvedere by Virginia Water for a weekend.

By the time George VI had been installed in his elder brother's place, there could be felt an underlying anxiety beneath the carefree buzz of London. The scene in the West End became hectic; people were even more bent on having a good time while they may. Cinemas, theatres and dance halls were crammed and doing a roaring trade. Everyone

21

pretended to ignore the war clouds that were gathering over Europe. And all the time Mr Adolph Hitler day after day blared at us from our wireless portables as he continued to gobble up more countries as ruthlessly as a wolf devours lambs.

"He'll have to be stopped sometime," Aunt Dora declared one evening after we had been listening to more depressing news from the Continent. "Modelling in that shop isn't going to be much use if war comes. What about training as a secretary? You've had a good education and you've got a good brain. I think it is time you gave up gallivanting about and used it."

I looked up from my knitting. We were most of us great knitters in those days when much time was spent listening to the wireless. I always liked to have some work in my hands. I knew my aunt had never approved of my modelling, or rather had thought it a waste of brain power which she was convinced I had, though I could not see it. Now, as I glanced up at her, all of a sudden I noticed how aged she had become, and my heart missed a beat. Was I going to lose her? I had never contemplated such a thing before. She was my only relation . . . my beloved great-aunt who had come to the rescue when I was orphaned as a toddler. Both my parents had been only children. Therefore I had no aunts, uncles or first cousins, only some distant cousins in Ireland whom I had never met. My parents had married late and all my grandparents had died by the time I was born. Just my dear old great-aunt . . . She had been nothing but kindness and goodness to me all my life.

To look at Aunt Dora one would not know the strength that lay behind the gentle quietness. She was a small, grey, shabbily-dressed woman from Irish gentry; married before the Great War to a London solicitor. She was so unassuming as to be almost invisible. Only the few who knew her well knew how splendidly and supremely sensible she was. She had coped with the various large and small crises in my life with total unfussy firmness. She had always been invincible. Now she appeared to me faded, vulnerable.

"Yes," I said slowly while thinking my thoughts about her. "Yes, I'd better do that if there's going to be war, Aunt Dora."

And so it was that after a year of working my hardest, and finding that my rusty brain when well-oiled with homework really could rise to the challenge, I passed out top of my class for that year from St James' Secretarial College opposite the tall grey walls surrounding Buckingham Palace.

When I had started my training I had seen that, for it to be a success, I would have to give up going out so much, in fact late nights during mid-week were *out*. Almost fortuitously John was posted to India during my first term. He left declaring I was not to get married in his absence. I missed his jolly, good natured face and often wished him back, but nevertheless was glad he was not there to distract me with invitations.

When the head of the college called me in to congratulate me on my final marks, she suggested I apply to the War Office for work.

"They require a high standard and you've done very well," she praised. She was known to us students as a right old battleaxe who, if we slacked off, could devastate us with her cynical remarks. I flushed with surprise as much as pride. Her suggestion sounded a good idea. My aunt approved, and I went for a preliminary interview and then a second one, after which I was offered the lowliest of typing jobs with the lowest of salaries. Somewhat squashed by this – I would not even be required to exercise my shorthand nor any of my languages – I returned home to have a good old grumble about my wasted talents to Aunt Dora.

I let myself in and as usual called out to her. There was no answer. Knowing that she never went out at that time of late afternoon, I was seized with a premonition that something terrible had happened. Trying to reassure myself that perhaps she was resting, I went into her bedroom. Not there. In a panic I opened the bathroom door thanking God that over a year ago, when I had first noticed her deterioration, I had forbidden her to lock herself in.

I found her on the floor half propped up against the bath tub. She looked deathly ill. She did not move as I came in and I thought she was dead. I bent down, and, as my figure loomed over her, I could see the relief in her eyes. I spoke to her but she was unable to answer. Instead, and very bravely, she gave me a twisted smile.

In that moment I grew up.

Chapter Three

With my aunt's illness my life changed completely. The nursing home and doctor's fees were so heavy that the daily woman who had cooked for us, and always left an evening meal ready, had to go.

Except for an occasional outing with Denys, I dropped all social engagements. After work I rushed to stay with my aunt for the evening until the nurses settled her for the night. Then I went back to the flat, opened a tin of baked beans or grilled some cheese on toast, ate an apple and went to bed too tired and worried even to think of Gough.

At weekends I spent some time in the morning, and then again in the afternoon, with Aunt Dora. In between I did the chores in the flat, washed clothes and her night-gowns by hand in the bath tub, wrote one or two letters and paid bills.

Aunt Dora's late husband's firm of solicitors arranged for me to have power-of-attorney after I became of age in the summer of 1938. I watched anxiously the substantial bank balance she had built up through her own prudence being eroded by the nursing home expenses. My aunt was bedridden in all for eleven months. To begin with she did improve sufficiently to sit up in a chair, speak quite coherently and use one hand to feed herself. I brought her grapes and peaches to augment the stodgy nursing home diet, and I read to her, usually her favourite Jane Austen books. I also tried to thank her for all she had done for me. I felt I thanked her rather badly and rather too late, for by then she was sleeping most of the time and fading fast.

In the early hours of one morning (why do people always die in the early hours?) a hand written message was pushed through the door of the flat. I dressed, and with dread for the unknown went round to the nursing home. I was taken up by the night sister to my aunt's room. I had never seen a dead body before and I was shocked by how quickly death took over to shrink and wither. Just a little crimpled grey old lady with white head as small as a child's, sharp pinched features, and dull sockets in place of kindly, lively eyes. This was not my Aunt Dora. I left hurriedly. Later that day remorse set in that I had not in life shown her more affection and gratitude, and with the remorse came the tears.

The solicitor and his wife helped me over my ghoulish fear of the funeral. (My aunt had requested to be buried in the same grave as her husband). Only a handful came and all the while I could feel the coldness of her corpse in the coffin. It rained, but Denys was there. Dear Denys whom I had picked up in the fog. He took me out to lunch afterwards and was so kind and understanding that I would have married him then and there had he asked me at that point. John was in India, Dulcie travelling abroad. After a year, where were all the friends I had gone out with before my aunt became ill? Above all where was Gough? There had not been a sign or a sigh of him since the night of the Ball three years ago. Had I dreamed it? Certainly I must have read far more into his words than was intended, for had he meant all I believed he meant, surely he would have found me by now.

The simple will was proven and my aunt's small capital was handed over to me after the solicitor's fees and the funeral expenses had been deducted. There was enough income from investments for the rent in Holland Park – I wanted to stay on in the familiar flat with Aunt Dora's possessions round me if only to keep me from becoming more disorientated than I already felt – and there was some money over but scarcely enough to live on. My salary was all important.

Therefore on the Monday after the funeral I plucked up courage to ask my boss for a rise. I was still classed as a typist even though for some time I had been taking down shorthand notes in the office. He said he would consider it, and shortly afterwards, to my gratification, I was upgraded and put into learning cipher work, for which conundrums I found I had a natural knack. This I equated with my ability to do crosswords – hidden talents coming out, I tried to boost myself!

Thus I was able to stay on at the top of the big house in the flat which had been my home for as long as I could remember. And I managed, but only just.

The hot summer of 1938 was nearing its end, autumn already showing itself in Holland Park with dry leaves falling from the trees to make a rustling sound on the pavement below my window. The soughing would wake me from sleep, a somehow comforting sound showing there was life in the world even if it was only rustling leaves that whispered to me in the nights.

Like everyone else, I had been issued with a gas mask which I carried to work in its box and kept under my bed at nights. I made black-out curtains and put them up on the windows. Outside they dug slit trenches and spoiled the pretty green parks with piles of muddy earth. They took down railings to use for machine parts in factories, and there was talk of children from the East End being billetted to houses in the country. Hitler was shrieking louder than ever over the wireless. Mostly I turned him off. There was nothing I could do to stop the inexorable process. We all knew war would come. The only question left in our minds was when?

In the long evenings as winter drew in, I had taken to doing the crossword puzzle in *The Times*, and challenging myself to finish it before reading the newspaper from cover to cover. One evening I noticed a column asking for volunteers in the evacuation of poor children, a project still very much in the making. The volunteers were needed for the Isle of Dogs district in the dock side slums of the East End, one of the poorest parts of London.

I typed a letter to the address, giving my particulars. A reply duly arrived. I hesitated. Voluntary work. No pay of course, but surely better than sitting in the flat on my own at weekends and getting all steamed up at the thought of the inevitability of war, with London most likely to be the main bombing target. Still, I did not really want to go . . .

What made me write to say I could report for work the following week? I do not know what made me do it, but for the rest of my life I thanked God that I had.

I had never been to the Isle of Dogs, in fact I had hardly been to the East End of London at all, but I made my way through Stepney and on down the West Ferry Road past the India & Millwall docks to the address I had been given.

I found myself in a narrow cobbled street lined on either side with identical mean-looking grey one-storeyed houses. Before me was a large brick building which looked from the outside like a warehouse. Under its grimed walls, in the cold and rain, stood a ragged crowd of women and children interspersed with dejected looking men wearing cloth caps. Many of the women wore shawls over head and shoulders against the rain. The boys wore jackets that showed thin wrists. Their shorts were loose and baggy. Some wore boots; others were barefoot, small girls too. All looked pinched with cold and most were snotty-nosed.

It was like a scene out of Dickens. I could scarcely believe my eyes. I had never seen anything like it before, and I found it difficult to grasp that I was still in London – *my* London – the great capital of a modern, well-educated, democratic country. What was the government doing about this side of it? I had read articles on the poverty in the East End, seen tramps in the parks, but had seen no photographs to bring the truth home.

Shocked, I made my way through the crowd queuing up at the door and shuffling into the building. The crowd, when they saw me, politely made way, the women admonishing the children and

29

roughly cuffing them aside, to 'let the lady pass'. The men touched their caps. Dressed in my black outfit as I was, I realized that I was instantly recognizable for a rich lady from the West End. I felt thoroughly ashamed of my garb.

On entering the hall a strong smell of onions and cabbage, mingling with the sniff from badly-fitting hissing gas stove heaters lining one wall, assailed me. The whole odour was permeated with the mustiness of old clothes. Through the murk of steam I saw the queue working its way up to a platform on which a tall slim girl, wearing breeches fastened below the knee over long woollen stockings, sturdy brogues on feet, was ladling out soup into bowls from a cauldron as each person came up. The way the girl was dressed made me feel more of a fool than ever in my smart go-about-town clothes. She was handsome, features aquiline rather than pretty. Something about her seemed vaguely familiar. I wracked my brains to think where I could have met her before. Italy? No. More likely one of the country point-to-points I'd been to. Another woman beside her was handing out thick slices of white bread, and beyond, in cardboard boxes, were piles of apples for the taking.

Once served, the people in the queue went to sit on hard benches near the gas fires where they drank their soup, dunked their bread, and munched their apples. When they had finished, in an orderly fashion they took their bowls and spoons to the kitchenette behind the stage where two helpers were washing up. Cups of tea came next.

When the jumble was declared 'open', there was a concerted rush for the tressle tables in the centre of the hall. These were loaded with clothes, each table sorted out into groups for men's wear, women's coats, children's wear, piles of jumpers and cardigans. I stood staring at a table laden with black boots: old used lace-up contorted boots from the smallest of feet to large size . . .

"Hello," said a voice at my shoulder. "You're Miss de Montefort? Good, I was told to expect you. I'm in charge – Dolly Crichton-Smith." She held out a hand. I recognized her face from the tabloids. Lady Crichton-Smith no less. Humm. So here I was with the rich snobby set, all of us doing our stint of good works! Well, it certainly needed to be done and who bothered by whom it was done when you had no shoes for your children on a wet day such as this, and not enough food to warm your belly? Still 'charity' was a nasty word, particularly if bestowed by ladies in furs and pearls. So far I had seen neither. Petite Dolly was dressed in a polo necked pullover and wide-legged slacks. "First time doing this sort of work?" she enquired pointedly looking me up and down.

"Yes," I said, "one's heard about poverty in the slums of Glasgow, but . . ."

". . . not on your doorstep!" she ended for me. "We're trying to make people more aware of the conditions. There's always been a great deal of unemployment in dockland, also a lot of drunkenness which makes for large families. In a life of grinding poverty birth control goes out of the window, not that it was ever in it. Marie Stopes hasn't penetrated here. To get blind drunk and have sex are the only pleasures left. There's one good thing about a war: no more unemployment. They'll all be called up, given warm clothes and be properly fed."

"They may be killed."

"Maybe they will. Better dead than living this miserable existence of hand-to-mouth and reach-me-downs, don't you think?"

I hadn't thought; in any case Dolly went rattling on, "Our headquarters obviously omitted to inform you about wearing suitable clothes. By the time we've handled the jumble and helped to fit dozens of shoes on grubby little feet, one's in need of a bath I can tell you! We're a voluntary society under the aegis of the Red Cross. Anyone is welcome to help. I gather you can come some days after work? Yes? That will be great. Some of us can come more often than others. We have evening parties periodically to raise money. I hope you'll come to our next. Follow me and I'll show you what I want you to do today."

She led the way through the hububb of women scrabbling through the garments on the tables for clothes to fit, some hair pulling and much elbow digging going on as chosen garments were fought over and sometimes ripped in the process.

"Don't you try and distribute . . .?" I began while watching an urchin kicking the shins of a fat woman who had snatched a jumper from him. The woman clonked him on the head. The small boy was fighting back with the bravest.

"We did at first. Impossible. Better to leave them alone. The jumble goes. We can never get enough shoes. What they find they don't want when they get home they can always sell for a penny a piece. A penny buys a nice bagful of sweets. Through here." My informant led me to a small room at the back where there was a table and typewriter. Leaves of printed foolscap paper were scattered about untidily.

"I've started to sort it out," Dolly explained, "but I keep on getting called away. Thank goodness you type. I can only manage with two fingers. You can get going straight away. We are making out lists in alphabetical order of parents who are prepared to send their children to the country to escape the inevitable bombing that will come with modern warfare. Here," she picked up a foolscap paper. "All you have to do is to type in the various columns the name of head of family and address; names of children, their sex and ages. I'll make an announcement and form up a queue outside. So far parents have been remarkably reluctant to come forward. Try and make it clear to them that there is no harm in putting their childrens' names down. If they change their minds, by the time it comes to the point they can always withdraw the names, but if they *aren't* registered they may find that by then there is a waiting list. We have to gain their confidence. They are frightened of a bureaucratic trap, and I don't blame them. Those that know us here trust us, thank goodness."

"I see. No coercion."

"Certainly not. It's their choice. One air raid will cause a stampede. By then it might be too late if stations and train lines are badly bombed. Okay? I'll leave you to get on with it. Give me a shout when you're ready and we'll start."

At the table I arranged a pile of foolscaps in each letter heading. Soon a line of rather suspicious East-Enders began to trickle in. I made each family sit down in turn. One couple brought six of their ten children with them. I explained the scheme and encouraged them to ask questions.

"You see," I said thrusting my shameful silk-clad

33

legs well under the table while the kids looked goggle-eyed at me, "there is no question of your children being taken away from you by force. Each family has to make up its mind whether or no they want their children safe from bombing. There will be the advantages of fresh country air and plenty of milk and good wholesome food on the farms. It is up to you to decide. I suggest it is only sensible to put their names on the list now. You can withdraw them when the time comes if you so wish."

"No strings attached, Miss?" the gaunt father of the ten wanted to know.

"No strings attached."

"Could we visit them?" the tired looking mother asked doubtfully.

"Yes, of course. You will be given the addresses and you can arrange visits with the foster parents by writing."

"*Foster parents* did you say, Miss?" the woman's eyes narrowed. I saw that I had made a blunder and that this was not a tactful term to use. "Them as takes in kids permanently?" she added.

"No, no," I hurried to repair the damage, "only foster parents for the duration or as long as you choose to leave them there. It won't necessarily be a husband and wife. Could be a mother and daughter, or adult sisters or a spinster. Anyone suitable will be required to take children into their homes if they have a spare room or rooms. They might even go to a mansion where there'd be servants," I extemporized warming to the subject I knew little about.

Again it was not a good move. "I wouldn't 'ave my kids looked after by servants," the faded woman sniffed. I decided it was better not to elaborate.

34

One man asked if the train tickets to visit would be issued free by the government, and if so how often they would be entitled to go.

"I'm afraid I can't answer that one," I said, stumped. "You see I'm new here." The withering look of contempt the man gave me was enough to quickly squash any preconceived ideas I might have had of the poor. No flies on them I was rapidly learning. The East-Enders of the Isle of Dogs had the edge on me every time!

However, despite my ignorance, my first recruitment attempts seemed to be going well from the way my foolscaps were filling up. I only hoped the government knew what it was doing in banishing the poor little blighters to become homesick no doubt. They would be sent to wide open country mostly in the south east, country that was the very opposite of the cramped, soot-encrusted homely cosiness beside a blackened range they were used to, with the soft downy comfort of a bed shared with the humanity of brothers and sisters.

I learnt a great deal from my first encounter with the docklanders of London, and I came quickly to admire the stubborness and wiliness of these people who despite their evident poverty were the very opposite of down-trodden. They gave me my first feeling of belonging. In that dingy gas-smelling hall I became aware of patriotism. We were Londoners all, all in the same boat, West End and East End about to face God knew what from air and sea. I even envied them for their tight units. When subsequently I came to visit them in their homes, I discovered that often three and sometimes four generations lived in their small back to back houses with a patch of garden for the washing line and the growing of vegetables, beyond which, against the back fence, was situated the closet. Yes, in a way I envied them.

They may have had to go out in the rain to use the convenience, but *they* did not suffer from loneliness.

Chapter Four

During a pause, the girl I had seen ladling out soup on the dais, came in carrying a tray with two cups of tea and a plate of sandwiches.

"I'm Babs," she said, perching on the table and looking about her speculatively while swinging her long legs. She munched at a sandwich, "I see you've sorted things out. Dolly's a gem but like me, she's awfully untidy."

"How long have you been coming?" I asked, helping myself to a second egg sandwich. "These are delicious. Who made them?"

"My turn to feed the helpers today. Lots of salad cream mixed in – that's the secret. I suppose I've been coming to the slums now for two years, since we had a tragedy . . ." she broke off, her hazel eyes clouding over. "I got hooked," she hastened on. "Dockers are a most entertaining lot. Wonderful cockney humour. We have some great laughs. The first time I took a trades union leader home, my father nearly had a fit! 'Red in tooth and nail,' he exploded. But after some neat whiskies they got on like a house on fire. Poor Dad; he's had to get used to my assortment of friends. I don't believe in class. Stupid; it's what makes people tick that's interesting. Dance here next; one meets all sorts."

"Here? In this hall?" For a second time that day I could not believe it. I was sure my aunt would never have let me go to a dance on the Isle of Dogs with a bunch of communists.

"Why not? In aid of charity. We raise most of the money that way. Locals on the committee help to organize the hop. We decorate the hall to disguise the shabbiness somewhat, and the men arrange the drink: beer and lemonade only. They wear their Sunday suits while we dress up like anything. It's good fun," Babs laughed in her uninhibited way.

I sipped my tea speculatively. What were the dockers like to meet socially? I for one would find it embarrassing dancing with the men who had touched their caps to me. And the girls all dressed up in their finery? Surely not. The prospect sounded to me more like a fiasco than fun.

"The committee consists of councillors and tub thumper types, all raring for reform, and with reason," Babs rattled on. She seemed to read my reservations. "They're awfully nice once you can get below the pontificating. Most are jolly good dancers; much better than our petted lot. We bring our own partners, and there hasn't been a brawl yet! Tickets are quite steep. The whole idea is to raise lots of money. There's a raffle and a buffet supper. I promise you the men are fine; I've never known them get drunk when the ladies are around. In fact, perfect gents. There's been a welfare society here for ages, but the deb set taking part is something new. Dolly started it and it's cottoned on. Beneficial to both sides, I'd say. Sorry, must dash to my post."

It was food for thought.

Meeting these people, both debs and dockers,

was an eye-opening experience for me, and the time passed busily and swiftly. Gas lights were lit overhead. We began to pack up and put things away. The hall had to be left tidy for the next event. What with Red Cross functions, the Salvation Army and other charitable institutions using it, it was in constant demand.

I was helping Dolly to stack the trestle tables when she asked me how I was getting back. "The way I came," I said.

"What's that?"

"Walk to bus and tube."

"Best not to be on your own in the dark in the docklands. Plenty of punch-ups. One has to watch out for opium dealers and the White Slave traffickers," Dolly warned.

"Humm. I read about that girl in *The Times*."

"She was fortunate. Found drugged and dumped on a doorstep. There was such a hue and cry it must have frightened the South Americans off. Her father was a Welsh Guards Officer."

"I'm not in that category. No one's going to bother to kidnap me," I laughed, my bitterness not far under the surface. Who would make a hue and cry for *me*? I could disappear without anyone outside the office even noticing. I felt sorry for myself and I hated myself for feeling so. I had been in this down-in-the-mouth mood ever since Aunt Dora had died. My only outlet was work. The rest of the time I felt dull and depressed. What had happened to the teenage girl who modelled lovely clothes and was always out and about having fun, the girl who had fallen in love with Gough? I was old before my time – passed over . . .

39

"I'm not so sure that they wouldn't bother to kidnap you," I heard Dolly say through my gloom. "You're one of the tall slim types they're after. Anyway I wouldn't risk it. Where do you live?"

"Holland Park."

"Fine. I'm in Bayswater. I'll give you a lift back. We'll drop Babs off on the way."

I thanked her, but it was hardly necessary. She was the sort of strong charactered person, rather like my friend Dulcie, who took over people like me.

After locking the hall behind us, we got into Dolly's car and, with Babs sitting in front, drove off. I sat at the back and only half listened to the two girls chatting away. It had been a long day and it had been a long week in the office and I had no food in the flat. If I was going to keep up this sort of thing, I would have to do my shopping in my lunch hour in future. I was sleepily thinking these thoughts when Dolly turned her head to say, "You'll come won't you?"

"Er . . . to what?" I sat up blinking.

She laughed. "We've been discussing arrangements for the dance in the hall. Can you make it?"

"The one I told you about," Babs added. "Next Saturday as ever is. Day off from soup kitchen and jumble."

"I'd like to but . . ." I hesitated . . . "I'm not sure that I can find a partner at such short notice." Denys had gone on holiday to Scotland to shoot. And there was another matter: Babs had said the tickets were expensive. It was no good kidding myself that I could keep up with this wealthy do-gooder set.

"Not to worry about that," Dolly said in her cheerful tones. "Not that sort of stuffy dance. Everyone mixes."

"There'll be plenty of spare men," Babs took up, "Angus is coming, and my brother."

"Who's Angus?"

"One of them," Babs laughed. "Freedom for Scotland from the English yoke and all that. I met him at the Caledonian Ball and fell flat, he's so different from the conventional types. Our engagement is to be announced shortly. With war on the brink we'd better get on with it – so says Angus."

"He's a super real braw Scotsman," intersperced Dolly.

"Oh congratulations." I offered my felicitations somewhat enviously. Handsome Babs seemed to have it all on a plate including a 'super' man to marry.

"So you can come?"

"Yes – rather," I said with a brightness I did not feel; then I thought: oh to hell with the money.

Dolly drove on down to the embankment at Millbank. The tall rounded street lamps shone in streams of colourful lights across the unsmooth river. We crossed Vauxhall Bridge to Grosvenor Road and then turned off to the right into the entrance of a large square set in a three acre site of lawns and flower beds.

"Don't bother to take me to the door. Drop me here," Babs said in her bouncy tones. We stopped by a pond with a central dolphin fountain spraying water. "See you," Babs waved a hand to me in the back. She left. I transferred myself to the front seat and we set forth again.

Dolphin Square, well lit up, a series of expensive riverside blocks of flats, each named after an English admiral, was soon left behind at the rate Dolly was driving her sports car, yet somehow it had caught my imagination and I went on thinking about it. I remembered the furore it had caused when built. 'Ugly high brown brick blocks ruin the landscape', the headline of an evening newspaper had read. 'Should never have been permitted. Sticks out like sore thumbs on the skyline of London; Pimlico and environment no longer a village'. I wondered if the wealthy who were privileged to live there in what was then considered to be 'the epitome of fashion' in swinging London, were more friendly than our lot in W11. Certainly Babs was friendly enough – and privileged enough to live there with its overall central heating controlled from the basement, its indoor swimming pool and sports facilities below, its shops, amenities, restaurant and reception areas for hiring out. But did Babs and her parents know their neighbours? Londoners were notorious for *not* knowing them. My aunt and I, after all the years in Holland Park were barely on nodding acquaintance with the people in the rest of our abode of flats; each was isolated by its separate entrance.

We sped on. "Which way now?" Dolly's voice interrupted my thoughts.

"Next turn left – and here we are." I indicated that Dolly draw up before a shabby grey front in a row of Georgian type houses. "I'm on the top floor; entrance at the back. The old servants' quarters," I imparted. I thought the society women had better know straight away that although I was glad to give practical help I was in no position to contribute to the funds.

Dolly screwed her head round to look up at the small top windows half hidden by a parapet. "Babs' flat is on the top of Osbourne House," she said. "Lovely spacious rooms and marvellous view. Yours looks rather fun too. Well now, plans. Be at my house at six next Saturday; no, say half five. Can you bear to put on your glad rags so early? Others of us will be there even earlier. Always quite a bit to be done at the last moment. Dance starts at seven-thirty and ends punctually at midnight. No dancing on Sundays in those non-conformist parts, thus Cinderellas all of us,' she chuckled.

"Where can I get my ticket and can I pay by cheque?" I asked hoping the sum was not too fearsome an amount. My electricity bill had just come in and must be paid first. There was no central heating in the attic quarters. I often used to think of the maids getting up in the dark on a freezing morning and dressing without any heating at all before descending to light the coal fires in every room in the house. My aunt and I had survived with the one gas fire in the main room and a series of electric heaters. Since her death I had tried to exist on the gas fire only; as a result the bathroom and my bedroom were like morgues in winter.

"I'll get your ticket. Don't worry about the money; you can pay me back sometime. You see I think you'll fit in with us, and that's meant as a compliment! So nice if you can come on a regular basis. Many say they will and then lapse."

"No, I wouldn't do that. I won't let you down." I did not add that I was intrigued to see how a mixed dance as described would work, and also I wanted to see Babs again. I *must* have seen her somewhere before. Where? It puzzled me.

Dolly rummaged in her handbag and produced a visiting card. "Here's my address and telephone number in Bayswater." She handed it over.

"Thanks so much for the lift. See you Saturday," I said and banged the car door shut behind me.

Once in my flat I made a cup of coffee and sat huddled over the gas fire in the freezing sitting-room. I cupped my hands round the warm mug and thought about the events of that day and the people I had met. Much as I liked the girls I did not feel we could ever be real friends. Our lives and circumstances were too different, too far apart.

I was not one of the East-Enders who deferentially called me 'Miss' and made way for me as if I were royalty, but then neither was I of Dolly's deb set, or of Babs' county set. I was a mere, very ordinary, in-the-middle, Londoner. I really did not fit in even there. Since my aunt had died my *raison d'être* – apart from my work – for living in London had gone. I had begun to wonder *who* I was and where I belonged – if anywhere. It was not a nice feeling.

As I warmed my hands on the mug and supposed I should open a tin of tomato soup for supper as there was little else in the flat and I really could not be bothered to make an omelette or scramble eggs just for myself, I felt not only physically cold, I felt cold inside, and not a little frightened for the future I faced alone.

My work isolated me further: it was highly secret. I knew too much about the ominous signs on the horizon as that Christmas of 1938 drew nearer.

* * *

There was still plenty to do in the hall when I arrived with Dolly. There were the multi-coloured streamer paper decorations to finish hanging; the sandwiches to be cut; prepared food to be carried from cars and brought to the small kitchen at the back ready to be laid out on oil cloth covered trestle tables. Bakelite plates were stacked ready for use, knives and forks gathered.

Some local men were busy assembling tumblers at the beer bar presided over by their committee. They all looked excessively spick and span in dark suits and well polished clumpy shoes. Their hair, cut very short, was well smarmed down with water. At first it seemed strange to me that none brought their womenfolk, but then, thinking back to the women I had seen at the jumble sale, I felt in any case most of them would have been too tired to come. Babs said the mothers were kept battened down in the home looking after the kids. She said she'd seen enough to ensure that she and Angus weren't going to have any 'bairns'.

I crossed the room to help Dolly who was setting up a display of expensive looking raffle presents. Near the entrance was a rickety card table for the selling of the tickets. It was a rush to get everything ready before the doors were opened.

Because I knew the hall to be a chilly place, that night I had put on a rather sophisticated long dinner gown with matching bolero for warmth. It was in black, slim-skirted and cut on the cross to hug hips; the bolero was trimmed round neck and short sleeves with pretty white *broiderie Anglaise*. The other girls were as dressed up as Babs had said they would be.

She, incongruously, wore a cardigan over her

décolleté ballgown: "Until the place warms up with the dancing throng," she shivered. I saw the goose pimples on her chest.

Guests began to arrive. Coats were piled in the lobby. Young men with their debutante girlfriends handed in their invitation cards at the door, each one of which was scrutinized by a six foot four Guards sergeant whom Babs said was in the Grenadiers. Knowing nothing much about Guardsmen I supposed he threw grenades. All the tickets had been bought previously. The Grenadier saw that no gatecrashers were allowed in which might have led to fights with the locals. High pitched nasal upper class voices mingled with braw cockney. The mix seemed to me odd. Yet why should it be? We were all of us British and on the brink of war.

"Oh good, there's Angus," Babs exclaimed at my elbow. She dashed off to meet a group of young men coming through the doorway, one of whom, presumably Angus, was dressed in a kilt and was greeted with a peck. She took him by the arm and brought him up to me.

"I want you to meet my fiancé," she said proudly. "Angus, this is our latest recruit . . ." She drew a blank and gave way to laughter. "It's too absurd; I don't know your name!"

"Isabella de Montefort. Bel for short," I responded nervously, always a little embarrassed at announcing the flowery name given to me after one of those Huguenot ancestor settlers in Wicklow, as I had once related to Gough.

Instead of chatting on in her usual inconsequential way, Babs stood staring at me until I was quite discomforted and glad to hear the six piece band on the platform sounding off for the first dance.

"Well, well, *well* . . ." after a while she remarked inconclusively above the blare.

"Come on lass, let's lead off," Angus suggested. He was a stocky, powerful chested Scot with a shock of red hair that stood up at the front in a thick matt. The couple took to the floor, tall Babs topping him, yet managing to look graceful (cardigan discarded!) with her swan neck bent to his ear. He was the very opposite of Dolly's tall guardsman type of partner. 'All sorts' was certainly the order of this evening. I wondered what Babs' father thought of his future son-in-law. Would whiskeys be enough to soften *that* mix?

Before I barely had time to puzzle over Babs' odd reaction to my name – perhaps after all we *had* met before – a small cockney stiffly asked me to dance. Though he barely came up to my shoulder, he masterfully pranced me off at such a pace that all my concentration was needed to keep my feet upon the floor. Neatly dressed in a well pressed worn suit, he yet smelled of fish, and indeed during the next half hour related how he *was* a fisherman: "Thames fishin', Miss, an' them scarcer than ever. No money in't nowadays. Estuary's only decent place left to net."

We sat out drinking beer and I heard more about fishing or rather lack of it. Up till now I had not known there was any fishing in the Thames at all. The moment the band started again several more locals loomed up in front of me. Apparently one was not in danger of being a wallflower in the docklands! I was enjoying myself. It was fun. The foremost man seized me round the waist and without further ado whirled me away. I had thought John Shawe an energetic dancer, but these men from the Isle of Dogs who bred large families and kept their wives firmly at home, beat him hollow!

I danced with several others, then, at a more sedate pace, with Angus. He told me he was a bankrupt land owner of a small island he'd inherited off the West coast of Scotland with a ruin of a keep which he and Babs were going to restore while living in a windowless shepherd's 'bothy'. "The smoke goes out of the hole in the roof if the wind's in the right direction," he informed.

"How's Babs going to like that?" I asked.

"Och, she'll like it. She's a sturdy lass." He also told me a good bit about 'the bonnie Prince from over the water' at which I searched my memory from my schooldays and managed to produce one or two informed remarks.

"I'm a conscientious objector," he announced later when taking me along to the buffet for a sandwich. "When war comes I'll till the ground for tatties to help feed the populace. I'll no fight for the English. Never. They'll just have to doo without me!"

"What does Babs say to that?"

"She'll go along with it. She knows she cannot change me. Dinna care much for blood and thunder neither."

"But, but what if the Germans come?"

"Och noo, they'll no git over the water!"

"I'm not so sure . . ." Quickly I shut myself up. I knew of a fleet of landing craft being prepared . . .

What with fishing in London and a Scotsman who wouldn't fight and apparently couldn't care less about the *United* Kingdom, and my knowledge of what *was* likely to happen, my mind was set whirling, especially after a slug of whisky Angus had offered from a flask produced from his sporran. Now I knew what they kept in the latter! I was fast learning about all sorts of things. I no longer felt cold inside in this company. To have answered that appeal for volunteers was the best thing I had done in years.

Whether it was the slug of whisky on top of the beer or not, I did not know, but there was a sense of excitement in me, as if on a wave of good fortune, a wave that was peaking all the time, a heady feeling of friendship and destiny . . .

After my time with Angus, Dolly asked me to take over at the raffle table to give the girl there a break. "Don't allow anyone into the hall without making them first buy a book of tickets," she exhorted.

"OK. I won't be a minute." I went into the dingy back premises to powder my nose. Peering into the cracked mirror I saw again the girl I had been before my aunt had died: rosy of cheek, eyes sparkling. "Whatever happens in the future," I admonished the face in the mirror, "you are never to let yourself get into such a trough again. See?" I smiled at myself and went out smiling.

I was sitting near the door at the rickety table plying my trade of chatting to the latecomers as they trickled in, and urging them to buy more than one book for the 'deserving cause', when I became aware of a figure standing in the doorway. He was not looking my way but was gazing round the room as if searching for someone.

I felt myself blanching, and I clutched the edge of the table for support. I thought I was suffocating, or

49

was this what it was like to faint? My throat became unbelievably constricted, and for what seemed an eternity I could not get my breath back. Then it came shuddering through my chest and I could feel the blood coursing through my neck and up into my face. I swallowed, and with shaky hand gave the correct change to the couple waiting at my elbow.

My wave of euphoria peaked and spilled over and I had to fight to hold back my tears.

Chapter Five

For there was the man I never expected to see again; the man I had long put away into my innermost hidden being. And I was consumed with sheer joy to have found him once more.

He did not see me but continued to search the room, and I saw that I had not been mistaken in my impression during that first short meeting.

Gough Nicholson was an exceptionally tall, devastatingly attractive male with deep-set brown eyes, slightly wavy hair, straight nose and longish face with full lips that played a *soupçon* of a smile at the corners when in repose as they were now. His ears, to a small degree, lay not absolutely flat to his head, thus giving him a rather endearingly boyish look. Yet he was a man now, a man of twenty-three, and he was not the impeccably uniformed officer I had met at the Sandhurst Ball.

This Gough was wearing a crumpled single breasted suit unbuttoned at the waist and baggy at the knee. Moreover from where I sat, the front of his shirt looked none too clean. The knot of his tie (Wykehamist I recognized from one of my erstwhile boyfriends) hung somewhat loose and askew. But even more odd, his handsome clean shaven face was smeared with black streaks. If he had been wearing overalls one would have taken him for a mechanic straight from the works. But here he was, a latecomer to a dance, attired in an outfit that had seen better days while the girls in the room were all dressed up to the nines, and the gentlemen slum-dwellers were turned out as spick and span as anything in their well-pressed suits and spotlessly clean white shirts with high stiff collars. The work-stained latest arrival, looking so different from the immaculate cadet of three years previously, yet was, to me, immediately recognizable.

I watched him with fascinated gaze. Apparently not able to find the person he was looking for, he turned from searching the dancing crowd and noted me sitting at the table not three yards away, my eyes bright with emotion upon him. If I had gasped on first sighting of him, *he* jumped. I could see the startled upward jerk of manly torso!

I smiled broadly. He looked so funny with his frown of surprise on his face. And I was smiling too at the knowledge that I knew him instantly. Oh yes, I knew him all right, and my first judgement had been correct: he was an extraordinarily charismatic man of magnificent bearing. I sat on there at the rickety table smiling for sheer pleasure. I did not care what happened next. For the moment it was enough to know that he was everything I had remembered him to be.

"Well . . .!" He spoke at last with authoritive gaze while taking a stride nearer to stand over me. He glowered at me.

"You *are* in a mess," I observed, the smile of welcome still on my face. "I wonder I recognized you."

"Where the hell have you been all these years?"

he accused, annoyance showing in the words. I could see his jaw working. He was furious with me. He remembered me!

"In London, where else? I told you I lived in London."

"What was the good of that when you did not give me a telephone number? I looked up all the de Monteforts in the directory – there weren't many – and got some dusty answers."

"I haven't *got* a telephone. Most people haven't. In any case my aunt, though born a de Montefort, had a different name. She was married briefly."

"Hmm. If no telephone, all the more reason for an address. How is your aunt?"

"She died."

"Oh God. I should have been around."

"Why around? I . . . I managed," I gulped. I knew he had seen the hesitation. Those keen eyes did not miss much.

"Is that why you are wearing black? It's too severe for you. I remember you in a soft salmon pink."

"I was younger then."

"Your people are always dying. Why didn't you get in touch with me?" he demanded gruffly.

"To where could I have written? All you said was that you lived in Dorset. A fat lot of use. Anyway, if I'd worn the pink dress tonight I'd have died of cold." I hit back, absurdly happy and at the same time cross at his personal remark about my choice of clothes. Black was smart; black suited my fairness – so everyone else told me. Black was for London.

"You could have written to our headquarters at Bovington."

"Bovington? Where's that? What headquarters?"

"The Tank Corps, of course."

"How was I to know that you were going into the Tank Corps when you didn't tell me. You didn't tell me *anything*; etiquette says it is up to the gentleman to get in touch with the lady," I tossed my head indignantly.

"Exactly. I'll have you know that for three years I've been trying to sleuth you down."

"Unsuccessfully. Not exactly a clever detective."

"A rotten one, I give you." His face relaxed into a smile.

"Here, buy some raffle tickets." I held up a packet. There were several people waiting behind him.

He stared at my ringless left hand holding the tickets. "Thank God for that," he muttered under his breath. "Ah, here's my kid sister."

To my astonishment at first and then understanding, I saw Babs launching herself at him in her gauche boyish way. Of *course*! When together the resemblance between brother and sister was pronounced in their tall elegant beautifully made figures and their aquiline looks, though Babs had light hazel eyes and she was fairer than her brother.

"You're terribly late, Gough," his sister accused. "It's really too bad of you. I asked you to come early to help move tables . . . heavens, what *have* you been doing? You look as if you've been working in the engine room of a ship."

"Only under the old banger," Gough looked ruefully at his sister. "First the engine conked out, then when I got her going again she blew a puncture on me. I had to change the wheel, all the time spattered by mud from passing cars. It was an absolute nightmare."

"Typical," Babs had to laugh. "Come along and have a wash. There's a sink in the back quarters. I see you two have met before." She stared at me even more curiously than before. I was still sitting at the table issuing raffle tickets and handing out change while listening rapt into the conversation between the two.

"Why didn't you tell me you knew her?" Gough accused his sister.

"Give me a chance. I've only just cottoned on to her name. Poor old boy," she turned to me, "he got teased mercilessly about his lost pick-up at the Ball."

"Enough of that, Babs," Gough said severely, not a bit amused. "In any case *you* can't talk. Think of the way you went on when Angus wouldn't come to the point."

"Oh shut up and come and wash. Look at your fingernails. They're grimed with dirt. I'm thoroughly ashamed of you."

"You sound just like our mother," Gough grunted.

"But the raffle tickets." I waved a packet in the air. "Aren't you going to buy any?"

"At our first meeting I told you I did not want to lose you the moment I'd found you and I promptly did. For sure I'll be back to buy raffle tickets, and no more disappearing tricks, please," Gough imparted.

"I won't move." I looked up at him with my heart in my eyes. "You'll be required to purchase several books to make up for lost time."

"I'll buy the lot," he grinned, and left in the wake of his sister.

It was a miracle! He not only remembered me, he remembered the words that had passed between us.

Lifted from ordinariness onto a high plane by this man's presence, I sat on at the card table selling raffle tickets and glowing with the knowledge that he had come back into my life. I found myself bathed in the bliss of a veritable seventh heaven.

I had never been happier than I was that night with the incredible joy of finding Gough once more when I thought I had lost him for good. Such luck in a vast metropolis like London was almost unbelievable, and in the slums of the East End of all places! To be told that he too had tried to find me was all I needed to perfect the evening. I basked in the blissful present of his simply being there.

He returned spruced up – except for trousers baggy at the knees – to claim his tickets, hair wet and plastered down with water so that it looked black and straight. His face and hands smelt of carbolic soap which was the only soap to be found in the hall. That evening in my elation I sold more raffle tickets and made more for the funds than they had ever made before.

We danced together once. He held me as he had before so that he could look down at me and talk. But I knew that the touch of our hands together spoke to him as much as it did to me. There was everyone else for us to dance with that night. To mix was the great idea. The time passed rapidly and people of different backgrounds quickly lost their shyness and became uninhibited as food was tucked into, beer flowed, faces flushed and decibles grew higher. The one time I danced with Gough, I saw at close quarters that, naturally, he looked more mature than the boy I had first met just turned twenty years; but the single dimple that formed when he smiled was still there, and when his hair began to dry it curled above his ears and kinked slightly across his forehead in the way I remembered.

Even when we were not together I felt his personality at hand in the room, and I knew, as I had known before, that he too was abidingly conscious of my presence. Perhaps most warming of all were the looks exchanged when our eyes met at a distance in a repetition of our first encounter. Only now we smiled in our delight that we had met again. Strangers still, for how could we know one another after two of the briefest of encounters? It was an odd, intoxicating feeling to be in love with a stranger.

I watched him to find out more about him, listened to the manner in which he talked with the local men around the bar. He laughed and joked with them and always there was interest and kindness in the smile that crinkled when he talked man to man and looked at them directly in the eye. He asked them about their families and the conditions of their 'living quarters' as he called their back-to-back houses. He listened sympathetically to their problems and grumbles. There was not a hint of boredom or condescension in his attitude. I had never met a man like him before either at work or out of it. I supposed that this was how he talked with his men in the army. Once again I perceived how he was so very much a man's man, a leader of men as John had immediately detected, and I marvelled that he could be bothered with very ordinary me full of uncertainty and unfulfilled dreams.

Though Gough danced with his sister's friends on the committee, he did not sit out with them as he had with me in the basement of the College, but invariably made his way to where the men were gathered. It was not, I thought, that he did not care for the company of women, it was simply that he preferred the fellowship of men. I felt unique and elated in that, apart from his sister, I was the only girl in the room whose company he sought. He had an easy teasing relationship with Babs to whom he was obviously devoted. I wondered what sort of relationship he had with his father and mother. I wanted to find out all about him, hear about his life right from his childhood days, know his ambitions, his likes and dislikes, his hobbies, what sports he excelled in, for with such a magnificent figure he must excel in some.

As the dance was nearing its end with an energetic 'Strip the Willow', the 'Gay Gordons' and finally a riproaring 'Gallup', *God Save the King* struck up punctually at midnight. I looked across at Gough standing to attention by the band, his shoulders marvellously braced. I thought that even in his unpressed suit he looked every inch a soldier.

As we relaxed after the National Anthem, and were standing around chatting in small groups, Babs said to me: "Gough suggests he takes you back to your place. Is that all right?"

"Yes, of course. Good. I was feeling bad that you and Angus would have to go out of your way to get me home."

"Well . . . we had thought we'd go on to a night-club straight from here. Besides, you two must have lots to catch up on."

"Yes," I said vaguely. I did not know how much she knew. Did she know we had met only *once* before, at the briefest of meetings? "How did you come to hear about me?" I ferretted.

"After the Sandhurst Ball Gough never stopped talking of the girl he'd met. We could not think why, as he appeared so impressed by you, he did not show you off to us. Then when it came out he did not know where to find you the teasing started. Poor boy. He was permanently pink about the ears! It became a family joke of 'find the girl, Gough'. You know how families can be. Beastly cruel."

"No, I don't really know about families, never having had one."

For once bubbly Babs looked serious. "We'll see about that, Bel," she said after a pause. She gave me a soft glance under her long dark eyelashes and repeated, "Yes, we'll have to see about that . . ."

Chapter Six

"I hope the old girl doesn't let me down again," Gough remarked ushering me into a 4½ Bentley Coupé which was quite obviously the light of his eye. He tucked a rug about my legs, shut the door and went round to lever his long figure into the driving seat. I subsided into the deep front seat feeling as if I was a pasha. I savoured the old leather smell mixed with the tang of tobacco, and ran a hand over the shiny wooden dashboard before me to feel its rich smoothness. I discovered subsequently, that, rather uncommonly for a young man of those times, Gough did not often smoke cigarettes. He preferred to wait for the time when he could puff at a pipe with his male buddies. I found a pipe 'manly', as we used to say, and if anyone was manly, Gough was. We purred powerfully off into the frosty night, tyres crunching, a cloud of exhaust left behind.

"I don't in the least mind if the old girl does let you down," I laughed in my happiness at being at close quarters with him in a car. "I'm certain you'd be capable of getting it going again."

"Mostly, yes," he agreed. "Since passing my final exams in Bovington what I don't know about a Rolls Royce engine is not worth knowing. Most of my training there was spent head inside a tank engine.

Rather nice to know that if the army decides it doesn't like me, I can always go and be a chauffeur to some millionaire."

The traffic was light and Gough drove fast and well. I watched the hands I already loved on the wheel. I had never had the opportunity to learn to drive, and I sometimes felt nervous when being driven. But not with Gough Nicholson. His whole personality gave out a supreme confidence. When on the road, as now, there was no fuss, no unnecessary impatience or swearing at hold-ups as John had been inclined to indulge in. I could see Gough doing whatever had to be done with calm ability. He would be the same in war even with bursting bombs and blasting machine guns all around him. Whatever situation Gough found himself in, I was sure he could contend with it superbly.

After having had to cope myself from an early age with the sometimes seemingly insurmountable difficulties and the petty irritations of inanimate objects, without a male to come to the rescue, and then, after my aunt died, manage entirely by myself, I had achieved a certain practical competence, but being with a person like Gough gave me a feeling of security that I had never experienced before. On that first ride with him I bathed in the luxury of being driven in a super car by a super man. I thought his parents must have plenty of money living as they did in both town and country. I knew from John how meagre a subaltern's pay was and supposed that to run a car like this his parents must give Gough a generous allowance.

"Bentleys must cost the earth," I surmised.

"They do when new. An old banger like this one,

which had been driven to destruction, can be picked up quite cheaply. Fine as long as one understands the workings of a—"

"Rolls Royce engine," I finished for him.

"Right! You've got the hang of it," he laughed. "I do 'em up and change them for a better one. This is my third car but I've become so fond of the old girl and know her tricks so well I think I'll keep her. One day when I'm a General I might have enough money to buy a new one."

"You'd miss not having to tinker with it."

"True, but by then I expect I'd be too busy."

"Your ambition is to become a General?"

"No. My ambition goes no further than to command my own regiment. That's the tops for most of us. Red tabs and staff work, however interesting, could never come up to that for me. In a regiment you're commanding your men; it's a unit; you know them all."

Gough appeared to be able to find his way about London as well as I did, that was until we approached Kensington from where I guided him the last bit up Church Street to Notting Hill and Holland Park Avenue and on to my door. Once there I momentarily panicked, as I had all those years ago, when I did not want to give him the address of the shabby flat at the top of a house which did not belong to us. What would he with his Bentley, his house in the country and the centrally heated flat in modern Dolphin Square think of my shabby chilly quarters? Would this ruin it all? Could he be that sort of snob? Well . . . I'd soon find out. I pulled myself together and invited him up for coffee.

"Lovely," he said. "Just what I need to keep me

awake for the return journey. I'm short on sleep. They fairly work us when training. I wouldn't have come tonight had not Babs been so insistent she needed me for her do-gooding."

I thought that by 'return journey' Gough meant to Dolphin Square. He must indeed be tired if he could not go that shortish way without falling asleep! I led him up the back linoleumed stairs of what had once been a large single house, and into my sitting-room where I switched on both bars of the electric fire an extravagance I seldom indulged in when on my own.

"It's freezing in here," I observed. "Keep your coat on until it warms up. I'll go and get the coffee." I would have offered him whisky had I had any. I made the coffee in the way my aunt did: fresh grounds into a warmed jug; boiling water poured over, stirred, the grounds allowed to settle for four minutes with a cosy on. It always smelt delicious when made this way and tasted as good. I took off my coat, put on a pink cardigan over my evening dress, and returned with the tray of coffee and a plate of biscuits. "That's better," Gough remarked, "better than black."

"You've got a thing about black," I said. "Haven't you noticed this one has white trimmings?" I mentioned it in case he hadn't. "Anyway, why don't you like black?"

"I don't mind it. My mother wears it a lot. I just don't like *you* in black. Too severe, and too funéreal. Makes you look like a young widow. You've had enough deaths in your life already in all conscience. I wouldn't want to think of you being in mourning ever again."

"I won't be. There's nobody . . ."

"You'll get married."

"I don't think so . . ." I hesitated. I couldn't very well say that as nothing with him would come up to commanding his regiment, so nothing with me could come up to *him*, and . . . I noticed him smiling, "and," I ended, "war is not a time in which to get married."

"Quite," he said briskly, "yet it is the time everyone rushes into it."

"So if there's a war you wouldn't get married?"

"No. It wouldn't be fair. Now," he changed the subject, "please tell me about yourself. I've often wondered what you were doing these past few years when you vanished off the face of the earth. You have a job?"

"Fortuitously at the War Office."

"Phew," he whistled cocking an eye at me, "you dark horse. You know more about the army than I do. But well done. So; you have brains as well as beauty."

I blushed at the compliment. I could still blush though I had had my twenty-first birthday that summer. I talked a little about myself when he questioned me more. There was little to tell except that after my aunt's death I had gone with a party of girls met at the secretarial college to ski. "I found I loved it and that I was quite good at it," I said with truth. "I suppose I was a natural because I had learnt a certain balance by skating at the Queen's Club rink in Bayswater."

"Where did you go?"

"Tyrol. *Shoeplatter* dances and all that. What about you?"

"I go with the family every year. Usually February. Have ever since I can remember. Babs too, and

Ben . . ." he paused. "Scheidegg, Spiez, Berner-Oberland, Kitzbühel once when the Prince of Wales was there with Mrs Simpson and no one in England had a clue about it. It would be fun . . ." He looked thoughtfully at the red bars before him while munching at a biscuit. He did not say what would be fun.

I did not feel awkward with him in the silence that followed, though I was very conscious of being *à deux* in a flat at the top of a house in a room that was warming up nicely. Gough removed his great coat and I laid it on a chair in the narrow hall. We settled down again. Between sips of coffee he told me that after his initial training at Bovington Camp – the Royal Tank Corps Depot in Lulworth Camp where all the recruit specialist and young officer training was done for the whole Corps – he had been posted to Lydd to 3 Royal Tank Regiment, R.T.R. as he called it. I was beginning to get the specialized jargon. He now had his second pip and was a full Lieutenant, and he hoped in the not too distant future to become Captain and Adjutant of the Regiment.

"Lydd," Gough went on talking while I poured more coffee, "had once been a Royal Artillery – 9.2 Howitzer – station before the 3rd Battalion Royal Tank Corps, as they were then, moved there in 1923. I can't think why they chose it. Hardly ideal for tanks, Dungeness Beach being mainly shingle. Besides which it is absolutely in the back of beyond. Could scarcely be further away from civilization. Frightful marshes all round. We're always getting stuck in them. Am I being a bore? Do say. I get carried away by all this military stuff."

"No, no. Go on." I did not tell him that I loved to

hear it, all of it, loved to hear the deep masculinity of his speaking voice. Also, what he related was interesting from my job point of view in hearing what actually went on on the ground and not just through cipher messages. But what engrossed me most was the filling in of the picture of *him*, what *he* liked best. So far cars and Tank Regiments. Girls did not come into it!

"I gather you're an oarsman. How does that fit in with tanks?" I asked after he had told me quite a bit about Lydd and its remoteness.

"How did you know I row? Oh, my little sister boasting of my prowess no doubt. She watched me rowing for Winchester, and I rowed for the Royal Military College. No time for that lark since I joined the Tanks. I still manage to sail, though, when I can get home. We keep a small boat in Poole Harbour. I love anything to do with water."

I didn't answer that, never having sailed, but we went on talking and I turned off one bar of the fire. Gough asked for more coffee, "to keep me awake. Delicious aroma," he sniffed when I came in with a fresh brew. I noticed that he glanced at his large luminous wrist watch every now and then. Was my company boring him? Was he staying on solely out of politeness? He had said: "coffee to keep me awake". My euphoria evaporated. The truth was he was already tiring of me. I could ski but I could not sail and I was not clever or interesting enough to keep hold of such a man's attention – even for one evening . . .

"I really must go," he said. "It's two o'clock and I have to mount the guard at dawn." He rose, his great height looming over me.

"What does that mean?" I asked looking up at him, never having heard the term which did not come in my line of work at the War Office. What on earth was he going to do at dawn, and in London, at the time of day they executed people?

"It means that I am officer of the week and that I have got to get back and be all smartened up in uniform to turn out the guard – left-right, left-right, quick march and all that – in time to raise the flag, the bugler to play the reveillé. Actually once you've got yourself out of bed it's well worth it. Dramatic, and also moving, with visions of camps other than Lydd in the remote corners of the Empire being roused with cups of char!"

"*Lydd*?" I gasped, "the back of beyond in Kent? All that way? I thought you were spending the night in Dolphin Square! Anyway, tomorrow – today – is Sunday."

"We know little about Sundays being a day off. The ceremony goes on every day."

"Char?" I said thoughtfully, a word Aunt Dora had used a lot. She had been to India with the 'fishing fleet'. "Was your father in the army?"

"No. He's in the City, but my mother's people were soldiers for generations. She's the one who inspired me. North-West Frontier and all that. Great stuff." He reached for his coat in the hall and began to struggle into it. Great coats being excessively heavy, I helped him to put it on which gave me a nice feeling of possessiveness, if not intimacy.

"Thanks," he said, "and thanks for the coffee. I must have drunk you out of house and home."

"What happens if the car breaks down again and you're late?" I teased.

"The dear old banger shouldn't let me down now I've tinkered with her, that is unless I have another puncture and then I would really be in the soup. I only have the one spare, which is already a gonner. If I'm late I'll be in the dog house and up for a drubbing before the Colonel with a warning that if it happens again I'll be cashiered, and all because of *you*! Being late on guard is a *very serious offence*, I'll have you know."

"Help! You'd better go," I exhorted, aghast that he had risked taking me home and then to sit drinking coffee for nearly two hours when so much was at stake.

We clattered down the steps double quick.

"Cheerio," Gough said. "I'll be in touch." And with that he leapt into the car which started up at the first touch. He roared off into the night.

I listened until I could hear the engine no more, and then I returned to the flat stunned and thrilled. He had *not* been bored with me nor was he snooty about my living conditions. He was not only as nice as I remembered him from three years ago, but nicer. He said the right things, did the right things, appreciated my coffee all naturally and charmingly. It wouldn't have mattered what 'class' or what nationality he was born into, he would have been the same: a true, through and through *gentilhomme* as they called it at the Lycée – a true man of honour . . .

He had acted in the flat in the same friendly manner as on our first meeting. He had not made a pass at me or even attempted to kiss me good-night in the usual way of boyfriends. As a result I trusted him implicitly. His rugged open face was the most dear thing I had ever encountered and I was headily in love with him. And the ghastly part was that he was a regular in the army and that stupid 'peace in our time' document brought home with such high hopes in the autumn by the Prime Minister, Mr Chamberlain, was worth less than the paper it was written on. There was bound to be war now, and Gough would be up to the eyes in it right from the very beginning. He was already training extensively for it in the career he had chosen for himself above all others in the footsteps of his mother's military line, a career he was manifestly suited for.

He was the strongest man both physically and mentally I had ever met, and because he was a leader of men he would be right out there in the front where the bullets flew the thickest.

And out there he would be just as vulnerable to the flying bullets as the weakest or most cowardly of men. In fact leading from the front as he invariably would, *he* would be the one to draw the fire, *he* more vincible to injury and death than all the other men in his unit. It would be a terrible waste. It was so awful a thought it did not bear thinking of.

I blocked my mind to such dire visions of the future. I comforted myself that we were not at war – yet. It might never come. Something could turn up. Hitler might have had enough of walking into other countries. There could be a miracle to divert the nations from war.

Pray God war would never come. Oh God don't let there be war.

I would not think of the future but only of the

blissful present; know only that I had met Gough again when I had thought I had lost him for good; bear in my heart with total trust those precious words: 'I'll be in touch'.

Part Two

Chapter Seven

The 'I'll be in touch' came from Babs. She wrote inviting me to Great Oaks Hall for the weekend after next. 'No Isle of Dogs that Saturday,' I read. 'Come down Friday after work. Catch the 5.30 pm to Wareham Station. The Hall is north of there in Bloxworth country, no distance away. Somebody will meet you – oh, and bring an evening dress for a dance the next night'.

Excited by the invitation but apprehensive of what I was in for, especially if Gough was not there to ease me along, I dug out an old suitcase of Aunt Dora's and carefully packed in tissue paper the same evening dress I had worn when first meeting Gough. Also in went a short dress to change into after arrival and a pair of slacks with brogues should country walks be the order of the day.

Wearing a heather-coloured tweed coat and skirt – which I thought Angus would approve of as much as Babs – I was duly met at Wareham Station, not by Gough in the Bentley, nor even by Babs, but by a uniformed chauffeur who seemed to know I was the guest without having to ask. Admittedly not many women got out with the bowler hatted City men.

"Cotton, Miss," he introduced himself and without further ado took my suitcase from my hand and led me to a polished dark blue Wolseley where I sat grandly in the back, though not in silence. Cotton liked to chat.

"First time to these parts, Miss?" he enquired.

"First time to any country house. I confess I'm a bit nervous," I said, thinking I would probably be more cosy with Cotton and his wife in a cottage.

"Oh you needn't be that, Miss. Very nice family. I was with the Major in the war. Now it bleedin' well – pardon my language, Miss – looks as if there's going to be another."

"I know. Isn't it dreadful. Did you say 'Major'? I didn't know he was also in the army."

"War-time. Called up like I was, Miss. We were together all through. He was wounded at Cachy, 1918. Whippet Tanks they were. We destroyed a group of M.G. Posts and then charged in close order for an attack. Tank got hit as we were dispersing the Hun. Caught on fire; terrible end for those trapped, but we got the Major out."

I shivered at the scene. "And after all that Mr Nicholson was pleased when his son wanted to join the Tanks?"

"Pleased and proud, he was. Mrs Nicholson too seeing as she comes from a military family. I wouldn't be so happy meself if I had a son, not if it's going to be another cannon fodder war like last."

"Will you be called up again?"

"No Miss. Passed the age, both of us. But you bet the Major and I will arm ourselves. Plenty of shooting guns in the downstairs gents, and if short of those, pitch forks from the farm 'll do. If the Hun navy dares to turn up in Poole Harbour, we'll be there to bash in their ruddy faces, that's for sure."

In the dark I could see little of the countryside we were passing through, but the big headlamps, shining onto the narrow roads, picked out dozens of rabbits mesmerized by the glare. Rather than slowing down, Cotton accelerated straight into them, though they were far too quick to be run over. "Shoot the lot on sight, the varmits," he muttered, "they're nought but a bloody nuisance. Gamekeeper traps them in hundreds. Scream the nights through they do like men on wire in trenches. Make good eating though."

I was pondering on the blood-thirstiness of man for man or beast when the Wolseley turned in between identical wood-beamed lodges, and on down a long drive lined with ancient oaks. We passed what looked like a bowling green fenced on one side by a grand old yew hedge. The car crunched round on gravel to come to rest before an 18th century manor house, high chimneyed, its edifice of weathered brickwork and seasoned beams low and baronial looking.

"How picturesque!" I exclaimed at the shadowed picture it made in the car's lights. "Tudor and Jacobean is it?"

"Yes Miss." Cotton looked pleased at my praise. "The first Earl of Dorchester lived here so they say. The Major is related to them. My grandfather worked in Lord Dorchester's stables. Oh, there's plenty of beautiful old houses in Dorset you'll find, Miss. You should see Milton Abbas and the Winterbournes." He got out to open the car door for me. "Can I have the key, Miss?" he asked.

The key? What key? "Oh . . . no key," I replied, embarrassed. As far as I knew my aunt's old suitcase had never had a key. I alighted and walked towards an imposing front door which opened before me. "Thank you," I turned to Cotton, but he was already in the car and driving off round the building. I supposed these servants knew what they were doing with my suitcase though I was not too sure.

A butler stood waiting on the steps, a stocky man in a black suit with stiff high collar. He greeted me with a little nod of the head and ushered me into a large and dimly lit oak-pannelled hall where the parquet floor was covered in oriental rugs. High up a minstrel's gallery overlooked the room. I was led through this hall into another large room where a fire burnt in a huge stone grate giving out the tangy scent of seasoned wood logs. Two large black labradors lifted their heads at me and growled lazily without getting up, while a low-swung dachshund rushed up yapping hysterically.

"Come here, Patty. Stop it at once now silly girl." A small woman rose from one of the deeply winged chairs by the fire. She came towards me hand outstretched. Her brown hair, heavily streaked with grey, was neatly parted in the centre and plaited into telephone coils around her ears. Dressed severely in black, she looked like something out of a Victorian print.

"Miss de Montefort? Barbara's friend?" she approached. "How very good of you to come all this way on such a cold winter's evening."

"I've been looking forward to it," I said releasing her doll-like hand.

"Our home has its drawbacks, but we love it. It is fearfully draughty in winter, you'll find. Almost impossible to keep warm. We shut the main rooms up after Christmas and hibernate in Dolphin Square for the worst of the winter months. Come and sit by the fire Miss de—"

"Isabella, please, or just 'Bell'."

"Ah yes, of course, Isabella," Mrs Nicholson mused. "Such an unusual name. I like its resonance and shall not shorten it as the young do – Babs, Ben . . . ah Ben. Fortunately they cannot shorten 'Gough'. Dear Gough. So you are the mystery girl. How he was ribbed when he could not find you, and what an extraordinary coincidence you working with Babs. You made a great impression on both and I can see why. Do take a seat by the fire," she gestured prettily to the chair over the other side. We sat down and she took up the tapestry embroidery she had been working at.

The room was centrally carpeted and instead of being panelled it had faded material on the walls from which hung a great many dark portraits. Like the hall it was dimly lit from pools of light, under one of which Mrs Nicholson sat, neat head bent to her work. A carpet by the door billowed in the floor draught, and a puff of smoke from the chimney gusted into the room. "See what I mean?" she observed.

"What are you making?" I enquired while thinking, so this is Gough and Babs' mother. Who would believe it possible that such a little person could produce such giants? She was dainty in the extreme, rosy-cheeked, and with a sweet, rather sad expression. The only facial likeness that I could see to Gough were the deep-set brown eyes.

"For the dining-room chairs which, after centuries, have worn out. I'm working exact replicas. Twenty-four of them. A mammoth task – quite daunting. My life's gift to the Hall! I suppose I'm about half way through. Now tell me about yourself, dear Isabella. I understand that since your great-aunt died you have been living on your own in Holland Park? That's not good for a girl of your age."

I did not immediately answer. I did not want to tell her that I had few friends, but she went on talking. ". . . I know how you must feel as I too was left an orphan. My father, following in *his* father's footsteps, was killed in a skirmish on the Frontier of India, but my grandfather survived through many such in the last century and came to retire near here. Hence my meeting with my husband in the baronial hall." She gave a tinkle of a laugh. "As a little boy Gough lapped up the grandparent's tales. I hoped he'd join the Indian Army, but he's so mechanically minded he prefers tanks to horses. Anyway, nearly all the horses have gone now. One does one's best for one's children . . . then they die or get killed in wars. You're very good looking. I expect you'll get married young."

I smiled, amused at her tone. Having met Gough I could never marry another and *he* was in love with his cars and tanks! "I'm happy in my job for the time being, and quite ambitious," I said, not wanting her to think I was going to take her Gough away – just yet.

"That's good you have interesting work. Women will be called up. They will have to go into factories and fields in the next war. You are better employed at the War Office. They have their eyes on Geoffrey there for a job – should war come. It's important for women to have a family, but then . . . they can be taken away as my third child was, Benjamin, four years younger than Barbara. He died last year at school." Her lower lip trembled. "Meningitis. Ill for only three days; that's all; he was the strongest of boys; so like Gough."

"I'm so very sorry," I said leaning forward in my chair. I would have liked to touch her in a gesture of sympathy but felt it would be presumptious after such a short acquaintance. So her Benjamin had died in 1936, a year after I had met . . . "Gough didn't tell me," I went on. "Nor Barbara. I did not know they had a brother." But I thought to myself: she's in deep mourning still. No wonder Gough does not like black.

"No, neither can talk about it. They were devoted to him, their 'kid brother' as they called him. Gough was so proud of him. They were both giants; oarsmen at Winchester; athletic like all the Nicholsons. Gough was like a second father to Benjamin; he led him and encouraged him all the way from a little boy through to public school."

"Gough is a leader of men," I said repeating John's words spoken on our first meeting. My heart went out to this small, gentle woman, shrunk into her large chair. When I entered the Hall I thought this family had everything anyone could wish for. They had health, the finest of physiques, intelligence, money, a lovely home, relations, friends, servants – they had it all and I almost grudged such abundance. Now I saw how tragedy lurked through even the most privileged lives, and those that had it all had more to lose . . .

Mrs Nicholson seemed not to have heard my remark about Gough being a leader. She was talking on: ". . . would have been a great sprinter if he had lived to fulfil his potential. Clever at his books too, more intellectual than Gough. He was destined for Oxford. His death hit Gough very badly. And Barbara too. It was to drown her grief that she dived into the charitable work in the East End through her friend Dolly Crichton-Smith. Angus does not fit in with what we had in mind for her. The two seem to us to have nothing in common. Geoffrey cannot abide him. Barbara has always been strong headed." She sighed. "You've met Angus? What did you think of him?"

"I liked him," I answered truthfully.

"You're the first person who has said that. Repeat it to Geoffrey, please. Perhaps your presence . . . you must come down again, my dear. Now, I'm sure you're wanting to get to your room. Just the three of us and a simple supper tonight. Barbara should be back soon. She's out visiting some cottagers on the estate."

"Gough? Is he . . . ?" I could not resist asking.

"He'll be arriving in the early hours, I expect. I do not like all this night driving from Lydd, especially at the rate he goes. Not long to wait now until he's posted to nearer here, thank God."

Mrs Nicholson led me through the hall and up a wide polished staircase where a great many more ancestors looked down on us from old black frames. We crossed the gallery landing and walked along a dark passageway to a door opening onto a small room facing away from the drive.

"The Rose room," Mrs Nicholson declared. "Over the kitchens and therefore the warmest in the house."

"How nice," I said, admiring the decor of rose patterned curtains and a thick deep rose carpet reflecting the light from a coal fire glowing from the grate. "My . . . my suitcase?" I looked round for it.

"That's all been taken care of. Daisy, the house-maid, will have unpacked it and put your things away. The gong will go for dinner in an hour's time but come down before for a sherry. The bathroom's directly across the passage, and the closet's next door. One thing we *do* have in this old house is piping hot water." She smiled and slipped out of the room.

Though obviously I relished being invited to stay in the luxury of the old Hall, Gough and Babs' home, with its soft-footed servants, its log fires, rugs and deep carpets so different from my threadbare abode, I yet found it a dark and rather gloomy place, even depressing in its over-poweringly panelled walls and heavy black mahogany furniture, not to mention the obvious sadness left by the tragedy of the loss of the younger son. Oh dear! What would dinner be like with the three of us rattling around in yet another large dark and cold room?

I took a bath across the way, finished dressing, and was trying to pluck up courage to descend before the gong went, when there was a tap on the door and in bounced Babs. With her entrance the whole atmosphere changed.

"Hurrah, you actually got here!" she exclaimed as if I had arrived from the other ends of the earth. She gave me a peck on the cheek. "Are you ready? Come, I'll show you my doss."

Along the same corridor we entered a large room with three heavily curtained windows. Clothes lay strewn around in untidy heaps intermingled with shoes, books, albums, ski sticks and toys. A gaggle of worn teddy bears and dolls lay on the bed. I sat amongst them as Babs changed. This was quite an education. She slipped out of trousers and shirt leaving them where she had stepped out of them. Then she picked up from the floor and put on a dress; she rummaged around in a drawer stuffed with underclothes until she found a pair of silk stockings that matched. Lastly she put on court shoes that were actually in place at the bottom of a cupboard. Vigorously she brushed her hair before the mirror and applied some lipstick all the time chatting away about the characters she'd been visiting in the cottages. The undressing and dressing was done in a few minutes and there she was standing in the middle of the room looking immaculately groomed. The dress wasn't even crushed!

"How do you do it?" I asked.

"Do what?"

"Look as if you'd just come out of a band-box, instead of which . . ."

". . . off the floor!" she laughed, shrugging her shoulders.

It was something to do with generations of breeding, I thought to myself. That tall broad shouldered and slim hipped figure would look elegant in anything, even when digging up tatties in old corduroy trousers.

On the way down Babs pointed out Gough's room. "Ben's is next door," she said with a sad little smile. "Mother keeps it exactly as it was; his bed is made up surrounded by all his school things, his oars, his hobbies. Morbid. I wish Mother would pull herself together."

"She's such a sweet person," I remonstrated. "It's not long. Give her time."

"Sometimes I think time's running out fast for all of

us with this talk of war. Pa can't stand the gloom down here. He stays in London more and more. They'll be fine when Mother goes up after Christmas. Basically they are devoted, but men have their limits. I lured him down this weekend away from his paramours, by telling him a pretty face was coming to stay. He'll be here early tomorrow. Likes to ride before breakfast and then golfs. Don't worry, he won't try and pinch Gough's girl! And don't look so shocked at paramours. Why not? Purely mechanical to a man like Pa. He and his men friends have a sort of set up."

"In respectable Dolphin Square?" I asked shocked.

"Good heavens no," Babs laughed heartily. "Somewhere near Regent Street, I think. He introduced the boys to the salon too. Said it was better to be initiated there rather than some cheap sex parlour where they'd risk getting the clap."

"*Both* the boys? Ben was only . . ." I didn't even know what 'clap' stood for.

"You look horrified! Half the public schoolboys are men at fourteen, said to be the most randy age of all. Gough is very fastidious. He never went back."

"But, you wouldn't want Angus . . .?"

"No, once married I wouldn't. I'll tear his red hair out in handfuls if he tries!"

She would too, I thought. I looked at her in admiration from my small sedate, enclosed world. She knew everything. Was assured, worldly, outgoing, unspoilt. I hoped Angus was good enough for her.

The gong had gone and we entered the dining-room where at the end of a long table places were laid for three. Candles were lit and the unctuous butler waited on us as if we were at a dinner party. To begin with I found his presence standing behind us as we ate, somewhat stultifying to conversation, but soon I found I was taking no more notice of him than the others did as faultlessly he continued to wait on us.

Afterwards we played three handed bridge by the fire in the drawing-room. Later Mrs Nicholson went into the pantry and in an electric mixing machine whipped up what turned out to be hot and creamy Horlicks.

"Night cap. We always have it. Good for growing children," she announced whilst handing a frothing mug to me.

"I hope to goodness *I* don't grow any more or Angus won't have me," Babs grimaced.

"It *can* happen at our age," I teased. "Truly; I had a friend who spent six weeks in bed with rheumatic fever, and when she was allowed up she found she's grown an inch!"

"Oh gawd," groaned Babs.

Once in my room I climbed into my high, luxuriously sprung old-fashioned bed. Half sitting up and sipping my Horlicks I thought how lucky Babs was to have a mother as kind and welcoming as Mrs Nicholson. Turning out the bedside light, I snuggled down between glazed linen sheets, found a hot water bottle at my feet, and fell asleep in the blissful knowledge that tomorrow I would see Gough again.

Chapter Eight

Suddenly I was wide awake. The creak of a door. There it was again. A ghost? I could see the light from the hall widening and a shape, a man's silhouette, entering. A live ghost! I half sat up, afraid. Should I scream?

"What do you want?" I asked between dry lips, my heart hammering.

"Just peeped in to see if you'd arrived." It was the voice I'd have known from the ends of the earth. "Did I frighten you? I thought you'd be fast asleep."

"I was, and you terrified me. Are there ghosts in this house?" I said sinking back onto the down pillows. He had been smoking his pipe. He smelt tobaccoey.

"Only friendly ones." He bent over me to kiss me on the forehead and then sat down on the bed. "That's to welcome you to Great Oaks Hall. Have they been looking after you?"

"Yes; oh yes. See . . ." I indicated the Horlicks mug.

"Dear Mother. She's determined to keep us healthy." We talked in whispers in the light from the open door.

"What would she say if she found you in here? Would she approve?"

"Yes. Why shouldn't she?"

"It's . . . it's just that I've never had a man in my room before."

"Never?"

"Never."

"Quite right. I'm all for that. Only I am allowed in."

"No turning out the guard at dawn today?" I smiled, the warmth of his words with me.

"No, thank heavens. I shall probably sleep till all hours. That's why I wanted to make my number with you on arrival."

"Car went well?"

"Beautifully. I had the top open. Full moon. I should be strolling through the woods, not going to bed."

"Aren't you frozen?"

"Yes," he said and put his hand over mine on the counterpaine. His hand *was* frozen.

"I think you need a hot bath. What are we doing tomorrow – I mean today?"

"Don't know. Babs will have arranged something."

"She mentioned a dance. I brought the dress you first saw me in."

"That'll banish the years between. I can hardly believe after all you've put me through that you are really here."

"What about all *I've* been through? Shall we go for a walk in the moonlight after the dance?"

"Good idea; *without* Babs! Sweet dreams my long-lost one," he smiled and walked soft-footedly out of the door, shutting it quietly behind him.

I lay there and listened to the bath water running across the way and imagined what he must look like soaking in the old-fashioned tub. Michaelangelo's David, the original of which I had studied in Florence? I had never seen a naked man – only statues. What a particularly nice person Gough was. Even if I were not in love with him I would have valued him as a friend. And what a mixture: a leader of men, aggressive in training and war, yet as gentle as could be in a woman's bedroom. Actually, at that moment, I did not care what he was like or even if we never became lovers. No, I cared nought about any of that unknown. All I asked for was to be with him.

Minutes later – so it seemed – there was a knock on the door and Daisy the chambermaid, in a striped uniform and cap over white hair, came in bearing an early morning tea tray with thin slices of bread and butter which she put down on my bedside table.

"Good morning, Miss, it's a lovely day," she said while drawing back the heavy curtains. Winter sunshine streamed into the Rose room. Daisy collected a bucket from outside and knelt down to lay the grate with paper and kindling wood. A spiral of smoke curled up from the embers of last night's fire. She blew on them and then held up some sheets of open newspaper, and in no time a red blaze could be seen through. She added coal and logs, brushed the hearth, put the fender in place and got up stiffly to leave. Daisy, I learned, had been with the family ever since anyone could remember.

"What do you do next? More fires?"

"No Miss, this is the last one. I've laid Madam's, and Master Gough is not to be disturbed. Mr Cotton 'as taken 'is car round to the stables for a wash and polish. The Major arrived early and is out riding with

Miss Barbara. I'd best be getting down to the kitchen to black the stove."

"Haven't they got a modern cooker?"

"An Aga, Miss. Keeps the kitchen nice and cosy, 'but the old stove still has to be blackened. Cook does the weekly baking in it. Says sponge cakes don't rise the same in an Aga."

I wondered what red Angus thought of this set-up with elderly retainers, who had been in service a lifetime, still carrying heavy buckets of coal up stairs and lighting fires before breakfast. However, what Angus might think was not going to stop me enjoying the luxury! I sipped the tea – but not for long. The sun shining through the window was far too inviting; besides I could smell fresh coffee and the delights of bacon and eggs wafting up the back stairs. I looked at my clock. It was already after nine.

I dressed leisurely and descended in my tweed skirt with pink twin-set jumper – no black! – and went down through the silent house. I let myself into the dining-room. There, at the far end of the table, and in solitary splendour ensconced behind *The Times* newspaper, was an iron-grey-haired replica of Gough. Mr Nicholson put down the newspaper and rose to his full height which equalled his son's but was twice as broad. He was dressed in riding kit with yellow stock. Dark eyes examined me over half-spectacles. "Aha!" he exclaimed, "Gough's girl – not to be touched." He continued to look me up and down critically a couple of times more, then added: "And a damn fine filly."

"Your remark is a bit premature when your son and I have only met twice in three years," I bridled.

"One doesn't need to meet more than once – not in

our family. I knew Adele was the one for me straight off, and so apparently, worse luck, did Barbara her young man. Help yourself to anything you fancy from the sideboard, m'dear." He sat heavily down into his carved chair.

"I like him, Angus I mean," I defied, sticking to my promise, whilst I helped myself to a sizzling plate of scrambled eggs and bacon from a covered silver dish kept warm by an oil wick. I poured myself some coffee, and took it to a chair noticing that the seat covering was in tatters. Adele Nicholson's life's work had some way to go yet. Toast lay in a small rack before me on the table. I tucked in.

"The Scot's coming down tonight for the dance at a neighbour's. She's an old friend of the family. Wonder what she'll make of him; bloody communists," Mr Nicholson growled, "they'll be the ruination of this country. Supposed to be our allies but I don't trust them an inch not to rat."

I knew better than to further that conversation, and in silence breakfast proceeded. I looked about me, not having really taken in the room the evening before in the candlelight. Glassy-eyed stag heads gazed at me from dark green walls. A full length heavy mahogany-framed mirror reflected the room which had heavily polished wide floor boards upon which the two labradors lay eyeing me. One came up.

"They're as greedy as hell and will try it out on a newcomer. Don't feed them. Down Jumbo," ordered Mr Nicholson, at the precise moment Gough entered the room and the dogs rushed up to him, tails wagging. I looked up. He was dressed in grey flannel trousers and a tweed jacket that was patched at the elbows. The jacket gave the impression that he had outgrown it with the sleeves too short at the wrist. I thought that even in old mufti a figure like his looked magnificent.

"Good," he exclaimed standing in the frame of the doorway fondling the dogs and smiling at me. "For a long time I've been picturing you sitting there."

I wondered how he would greet me. I felt I knew him as well as if we were old, old, friends. It had been a handshake after our initial encounter on the ballroom floor; on our second introduction we had not shaken hands on meeting or parting. Somehow to shake hands with the man I loved would seem ridiculously formal. Last night he had kissed me on the forehead and placed his cold hand over mine for a moment. Another chaste kiss now? I watched for what he would do as he stopped fondling the dogs and came into the room: he lightly touched me on the shoulder as he went up to his father whom he kissed on the cheek. I was surprised to see the embrace, but I liked it. Men from the upper-middle land-owning gentry who had been to top public schools, normally did not kiss their fathers, at least not in public. The gesture showed me that this family were not conventionally rigid. And it also showed that Gough loved and respected his father despite the latter's 'affairs' on the side which could have caused friction in defence of his mother.

"Where's Babs?" I wondered when Gough came and sat next to me. He plonked down before him a generous helping of kidneys sautéd in rich brown gravy.

"Out riding still," Mr Nicholson answered from behind his paper.

"You ride?" Gough asked me.

"I'm a Londoner. Rotten Row is too expensive for the likes of me."

"You can have a quiet mount here if you'd like. You know, you don't strike me as a Londoner, not in the sophisticated sense of the word."

"We're not curiosities, Gough. All sorts of types live there."

"The girl's got spirit," Mr Nicholson peeped at me over his paper.

Babs walked in, riding boots muddy. "I'll take you out later," she said.

"I've only brought slacks," I protested.

"That's all right. I'll lend you something." I gave up. Evidently if you spent a weekend in the country you had to comply. I did not let on that I had ridden as a child. I'd surprise them on just how sophisticated a Londoner I was!

Adele Nicholson was the next to come in, pencil and pad in hand to check on the programme before visiting the cook in the kitchen.

"We're out tonight," Babs said. "Lady Clementina Tottenham's."

"You'll love her," Gough expanded. "Great old lady from Edwardian days. She's a childless widow devoted to the young. Babs and I used to go to her children's parties carrying our bronze dancing shoes held on by crossed elastic. Remember Babs? I rather fancied the way I pointed my toes."

"Not a patch on Angus," scoffed his sister.

"I'm off to play golf at the Club. Won't be in to lunch." Geoffrey Nicholson leapt to his feet at the word 'Angus', and left the room.

"He'll be with his cronies all day," Gough said, giving Babs a knowing look.

"Oh dear, I hope Pa's not going to be difficult again," Adele frowned. She sat down and made notes on her pad.

I did not enter into this conversation with its obvious undertones, but sipped my coffee and watched Gough finishing off his kidneys with obvious relish. I gathered that Mess food did not come up to Great Oak Hall standards. Despite the long drive and late night, he looked quite untired and extraordinarily fit after what he described as a 'gruelling two weeks of manoeuvres'. However gruelling, the life seemed to agree with him. I could see him in both his parents now; a slightly taller, much slimmer version of his father with his mother's dark colouring, natural charm and general sense of caring goodwill. In such a sunny, good natured man as Gough, he seemed to me almost courtly, old-fashioned, a knight of old. I thought his manner totally genuine. From the heart.

"Gough, I wish you'd get rid of that jacket," his mother's voice impinged on my thoughts. "You look like an outgrown schoolboy in it."

"I only wear it at home. Reminds me of halcyon school days, those carefree years of childhood! Besides, after all the spit and polish in the army I like a bit of shabbiness. I tell you what; I'll stop wearing it when you stop wearing black." Gough gave his mother a keen glance.

"But Gough . . ." His mother flushed.

"Oh, cut it out you two," Babs interrupted.

It was not until later I learnt that the old jacket had been handed down from Gough to Benjamin, a six-footer by then and still growing, and that after the boy's death Gough had taken to wearing it again. I then became aware that he had not got over his brother's death any more than his mother had, and also that Babs knew both were vying with each other in their emotions to determine that his memory should not fade. Benjamin's death was obviously a terrible blow to the whole family, but Babs and her father seemed to have come to terms with the sorrow better.

Later that morning Babs and I took it in turns to play squash with Gough in a nearby sports club where there was also an outdoor swimming pool and tennis courts for summer use. Gough of course beat us, but at least I was better at the game than Babs.

"You're jolly good – for a girl," Gough said condescendingly, and we laughed.

"You wait – I'll get my revenge at tennis. More my game."

"Ah, sweet revenge, Isabella. I shall look forward to being beaten by you."

Angus arrived for tea by which time Geoffrey had returned. It was incredible how the atmosphere changed from the easy relaxed mode of breakfast the moment Angus stepped into the house. Babs talked too loudly, Adele nervously, and Geoffrey sat sunk into a deafening silence while Gough and I valiantly kept up a flow of inconsequential chatter.

"Phew," he said to me afterwards, "thank God you're here to help defuse the situation."

"I suppose your father feels threatened. One can understand it: his only daughter taken away to Scotland."

"More than that; marriage to a left-wing chap who says he'll refuse to fight for King and Country. The whole thing is obnoxious to my father."

"What do you as a soldier think?"

"Babs loves him. That's fair enough for me."

I felt lucky to be taken wholeheartedly into this family, but then *I* was no threat. They regarded me as Gough's girlfriend, and there was no question of marriage. I could see *that* from dropped remarks of both parents. Gough, with his potential for a brilliant army career, would not marry until he was at least thirty. I would have to wait for him until my late twenties by which time I would be an old hag! In a way, too, I was envious of Babs. Whether they liked the bridegroom or not Angus was in a position and ready to marry, and after months of rows with tears from Babs and exhortations from her mother, Geoffrey Nicholson at last, and with very bad grace, had consented to give her away in a slap-up society wedding to be held in London in the spring. If it ever came to the point that Gough and I married, I had no brother to support me, nor father to give me away. No wonder I was envious!

"My dear children," Lady Clementina Tottenham greeted Gough and Babs in the drawing-room where dancing had already started, "how you've *grown!*" Angus and I were introduced as the respective 'partners' invited. Little blue eyes under a curled fringe and almost hidden in a plump pink-cheeked face, keenly took us in. "You must meet everyone," she expanded and proceeded to do just that, many of whom were old friends of Gough and Babs.

For the next hour Angus and I hardly saw brother and sister. They were obviously popular in the district. Evidently the whole house was opened to the company for the evening, and we two, bored with dancing with one another, decided to explore it.

We climbed up to the top floor of the mansion and peeked into all the rooms, most of which were under dust sheets. Others were box-rooms under the eaves with trunks full of pristine linen never used, glassware, porcelain, dinner sets, silver and goodness knows what else still resting in their cardboard boxes untouched from sixty or so years ago when Lady Clementina was married to the lord of the manor.

"What a treasure trove. Do you know what happened to her husband?"

"Haven't a clue except that he died quite soon after they married. She's letting Babs and I take anything we want here for our new home."

We went downstairs and I danced with several unknown men until Gough claimed me. "Let's talk," he said. He took me by the hand and led me into the library which we found empty. We sank into a deep leather sofa by the fire where a waiter found us and plied us with more champagne and supper eats. After which we both simultaneously asked for coffee.

"All this coffee to keep me awake," Gough yawned. "I seem to be permanently short of sleep. In action one will be lucky to get three hours a night so I suppose it's good for training. My fault when I go up to London at Babs' will when I shouldn't, and now come all the way here to see *you*!"

"We'd better leave early tonight."

"No, I'm not going to miss a moment with you. Tomorrow's Sunday and back I have to go in the afternoon. Nice that you're wearing the same dress I first saw you in."

"I brought it down on purpose," I smiled.

"Purpose for what?"

"To close the breach in between."

Gough gently touched my cheek. "Your face is all rosy from the dancing."

". . . plus the champagne! And with happiness. No more black."

He grimaced. "As you probably noticed, my mother and I are having a sort of contest of her black and my wearing Ben's . . ."

"Mourning is good," I replied. "It helps to heal. Let her mourn, Gough."

"Can it ever heal when such a young life full of promise was snuffed out before he had a chance? He really was an exceptionally talented chap."

"If war comes there will be thousands and thousands of young deaths." I shivered at the chilling thought.

"Yes. I may well then say thank God that Ben-boy did not live to go through war and be killed, or worse, maimed. Do they talk at the War Office as if war is inevitable?" he enquired.

"Pretty well so, unless someone bumps Hitler off. Even then that wouldn't be enough. One would have to do away with the whole Nazi tribe. Oh, don't let's discuss war," I entreated.

"It's my profession," Gough replied, soberly.

"But you can't exactly be looking *forward* to it?" I pleaded.

"In a way I am." He shrugged. "What's the point in being a soldier if you never have to fight? That's the test. No one knows exactly how they will react under fire until the time comes. There's the challenge – the thrill of it."

"What if it ends up being hell?"

"Even if it ends up being hell. Will you wait for me until the war is over?" He looked at me, an urgency in his eyes, then looked away. "Yet how can I ask you, or expect you to do that? You know how desperate I was after Sandhurst to find you again."

"Were you disappointed when you did?" I asked, mischievously.

Gough laughed. "Only in that you were wearing black."

"Tank Corps come first with you?" I concluded.

"Yes," he smiled, wryly.

"Well," I said slowly, "that's all right by me." It was my turn to laugh. "I can compete with Tank Corps, though not with sophisticated women."

"In my eyes you are the most beautiful girl in the world and I can't stand sophisticated women. To discover one's love . . . well it's a miracle, isn't it?"

"A miracle for me too," I said softly.

Gough turned to me and took both my hands in his. "And herewith I give thee my troth for life," he recited while looking at me steadily almost as if we were in a church. He kissed me, and we snuggled down on the sofa together and talked about ourselves as lovers do.

And that night late, after we kissed very sweetly and properly on the landing, instead of throwing myself onto the bed in an agony of despair for a lost love never expected to meet again, my pink dress crushed about me, I carefully took it off, folded it on the bed in its tissue paper, and put it away in my suitcase vowing not to wear it again, but to preserve it for ever as a memento of our newly-declared love.

Neither that night did I wash my face, for to wash it

97

would take away those first sweet kisses upon my lips. Unwashed, therefore, I climbed into bed cocooned in the heavenly knowledge that my love was returned in full and running over measure.

Chapter Nine

Once again my life changed completely, but unlike the loneliness of the first time after Aunt Dora's death, I found my life transformed into becoming part of a family. Apart from my love for Gough and the headiness of knowing that he loved me, Adele Nicholson became the mother I had never had. In her gentle way she declared that their home was my home. It was the nicest thing that anyone could have said to me at that time.

Family Christmas at Great Oaks Hall with Gough on ten days leave was the greatest fun with the old house burstingly full of grandparents (one from each side of the family) a great-uncle, aunts, uncles, cousins galore and their children. In the general atmosphere of *bonhomie* that Christmas day brought, Geoffrey seemed to temporarily forget his dislike of Angus and actually slapped him on the back in friendly manner after receiving a bottle of Glenfidich whisky from him off the tree. The tree stood high and heavy with presents up on the gallery. The bannisters before it were garlanded with holly.

Babs and Angus, Gough and I went to two regimental dances, one at Bovington no distance away, and another with the Green Howards stationed near Wareham. Gough knew everybody and everyone knew him, and I found myself drawn into his circle of exceptional young men, some in the forces, some Wykehamist intellectuals.

Every day I was finding out new things about Gough: he was extraordinarily energetic – one had to be fit and alert to keep up with him both physically and mentally. I loved his quiet wit which showed in his creased grin and in the lifted eyebrow when something caught his humour. We shared many secret glances. He was kind, the basic essence of any relationship whether young or old; he never hogged the conversation but listened sympathetically to others' troubles, thus drawing out the best in people he met. I never saw him bored, not even with his nonagenarian great-uncle who kept on repeating himself. He drew him into talking about the Boer War and was rivetted by the result. He was relentless in following up what he thought to be the right path, and I saw he would be impossible to turn once he had made up his mind on something. And he was religious.

This I found surprising, I don't quite know why. He was christened and confirmed into the Church of England as I was and went to church regularly as I had when Aunt Dora was alive, after which I never really thought about it very much. Going to Holy Communion with Gough was a revelation. (Angus wouldn't go, so neither would Babs). The parents came. We four walked the short cut way through the woods to the chapel in the grounds which the estate workers attended. Kneeling next to Gough it was obvious to me that he meant every word of the creed and prayers we repeated together.

Afterwards we went behind the church to the graveyard for Adele to lay flowers on Benjamin's grave. It was in a secluded, quiet place under an elm tree and overlooking rolling downs beyond a low wall. I felt very moved seeing Adele there her eyes bright with tears. Her husband put his arm over her shoulder and they walked away.

"What a peaceful spot," I said watching them go, "but so sad."

"Do you want to be buried?"

"I hadn't thought about it. Do you?"

"Buried here, next to Ben-boy, pray God."

"But please not until you are old."

He took my arm and we strolled back towards the long avenue of oaks in the wake of his parents.

After a while I said. "In this modern age of non-believers you are quite old-fashioned."

"I could say the same of you. Your great-aunt's upbringing shows. That's what instinctively attracted me in the first place – and the pink dress! I've always thought that people who don't believe in God must be incredibly hard and self-sufficient."

"I think of you as tough."

"No, you mustn't do that. I'm as fallible as the next man. I need something greater than man to believe in to keep me together. Without God there is nothing and when there is nothing men give up and give way. *You* are the strong one."

"Me? Never," I laughed.

"Not only strong, but very strong," Gough said turning to me. "Do you know, darling, this is the first time I've not wept like a baby at Ben's grave? Your love gives me strength. I need you to face up to what is to come. Finding you has made me superlatively happy. Promise me that if in war I change, *you* never will?"

"Change from loving me?" My heart went cold.

"No; in that I will not change; but in other ways . . . War, the things one sees . . . it is bound to change one."

"Dearest Gough. I'll always, always love you."

We stopped on the track and kissed and kissed again. We stood by the bole of an oak tree and he kissed me so hard I felt weak and breathless with loving. And then, so as not to be late for lunch we held hands and ran as children do with glowing faces towards the house.

But that conversation on the Sunday showed me another side of Gough, one I had not been aware of before. It was not just I who needed him: he needed God and he needed *me*. It was a humbling thought.

That night in my room I knelt down by my bed to pray for Gough and for myself. It seemed only prudent to keep God on our side with this terrible war approaching.

I went back to the War Office and Gough went back to Lydd. We did not see each other for a month, but there came a steady stream of love letters. I met Babs on the Isle of Dogs where we co-ordinated arrangements for the Nicholsons' annual ski trip in February which I had been invited to join. We were to stay in Kitzbühel at the Grand Hotel where Mrs Simpson had been with the Prince of Wales a few years back, only we in England had not known about the romance then. Gough took his leave from year to year for this family event, and I managed to persuade my boss to give me leave too. I think I would have taken it anyway. Luckily, as has been related, I had skied before with Dulcie and so was not a complete beginner. Angus declined. He was too busy on his island and anyway he did not care for skiing. It was to be Babs' last holiday with her parents and brother as an unmarried girl. We shared a room.

I stayed on the lower slopes to begin with, but, fit from the skating rink in Bayswater (and now with riding!), I soon got my ski legs back and joined the four in the boxy ski-lift up to the Hannenkham top and from where there were various return routes down the icy ski slopes. There was little snow that year and we were forced to go further and further afield to find it.

One perfect day the five of us climbed for three hours on our skis up the opposite side of the valley where there was as yet no lift. We lunched up there in the blistering sun of the high peaks, the air cold, a hot *gluvine* drink to curb my trepidation at the imminent steep descent.

"Just like the Gurkhas who take *bhang* before battle," remarked Gough, who had also had some to warm himself. He stayed with me and his mother while father and daughter whooshed on ahead. Adele went slowly in her graceful style and did not fall, but I came a cropper several times, and when I did Gough was always there standing over me and laughing. "You're getting better," he said, "only three falls so far!"

At the bottom he became very quiet and stood looking at the view as if he could not let it go. "I want to be able to remember it when . . ." he stopped. Adele and I exchanged glances and I too stared at the mountains now threatening-looking, black clouds

103

racing over the tops; and I thought: five of us hurtling down the slopes to our doom. How many of us will survive?

That evening, tired but happy with Gough's arms about me, dark head bent to my cheek, we clumped about in our boots in the tiny space of a crowded café floor to the rhythm of a dance band. Then in came the men in their *lederhosen* to entertain us in their *shoeplatter* dances. Manly slaps on leather thighs intermingled with the charming stolen pecks of kisses at the pretty Austrian girl dancers through an open window of entwined arms.

We never stayed on late as most of the young did. Gough was too keen a skier for that. He was up with the dawn next day for a run with his father on crisp snow as the sun rose mistily to spread pink flushed fingers over the snowy wastes. We women did not go out on these early excursions. Babs and I stayed in our room cosy under our duvets until the men came in glowing with exercise and enthusiasm to call us 'lazybones' and pull the covers off us; and we dressed in a hurry and arrived yawning in the dining-room to join them for coffee and croissants spread with slabs of fresh farm butter and lots of dark cherry jam.

That time in Kitzbühel when Babs and I shared, cemented our friendship and it was sometime then that she asked me to be yet one more in her train of bridesmaids which included Dolly and another of the Isle of Dogs girl helpers. She told me how before they had become engaged she had lived with Angus to make sure they were compatible.

"And were you?"

"Yes," she giggled, "he's a real big mon!"

I gathered it was a rather hole-and-corner business

as they felt they could not 'sully' the parential roof or the Dolphin Square flat.

"Gough hasn't . . ."

"No, he wouldn't. He's a purist, a romantic at heart. That's why you two are so gloriously suited. You live on a different plain from Angus and I. We can be pretty bawdy, like Papa. Gough takes after Mother."

"But surely Babs . . . I mean your mother . . . it must be hurtful for her to say the least, to know about your father."

"I think she's rather relieved! My father adores her, cossets her and treasures her, and she basks in his love."

I was glad to have had the conversation with Babs, and I thanked God that I had kept myself intact through those years when I had given up hope of seeing Gough again. Both John and Denys had made advances in that way, but I had never really been tempted. However, Gough's attitude sometimes puzzled me. When he embraced me, even that time he hugged me hard, body to body under the great oak tree, I knew he was holding himself back, and so I too held myself back though I would have followed wherever he led.

On our last night in Kitzbühel, the impending doom we had felt on that day at the bottom of the mountain was brought home to us. There had been an air of excitement and anticipation in the town with streets being decorated; Nazi flags hung from windows, black swastikas on white and red backgrounds. When we asked what was afoot, evasive answers were given. A gala perhaps? Musical evening? A welcome to the new mayor? Shoulders were shrugged.

We had finished dinner and Adele had retired early to bed, Babs too with her monthly headache, when Gough and I went out into the frosty evening for a stroll. There seemed to be an uncommonly lot of people about on the slippery streets. It was a dark night; the moon was hidden behind clouds. A fall of much needed snow was expected.

We reached the nursery slopes where a crowd had gathered, and were about to turn back to the hotel when we heard the faint beating of drums coming from up the hillside, flickering torches glimpsed between trees. We stood to watch. More and more people appeared, pressing us from behind and looking over our shoulders. Many of them carried swastika flags. We had heard that the new mayor was a Nazi. In some puzzlement we continued to search the slopes, then, from way up the mountain, we saw lights weaving in and out of dark tops of fir trees. The first echelon came within view and we saw that they were skiers, expert skiers, hundreds of them, a whole army. They were clad in black and they came nearer and nearer swooping down the slopes before us in great expert swathes, many holding flaming torch lights on high. A great many more carried banners – swastika banners. I shivered. Gough stood behind me, protecting arms over my shoulders as the crowd pressed forwards.

Here, right in front of us, the peaceful ski resort of Kitzbühel was being threatened by an invasion of S.S. storm-troopers from over the border. It must be. The border was not so far away and had not Hitler done it before without declaring war? The cry of 'Heil Hitler' went up from hundreds of throats in greeting to the black-coated men of burning scorching flames, grey smoke pouring. It was a spectacular sight and frightening, one with an alarming beat of drums and flaring flames, a smell of smoke and burning fuel heavy on the air. So sinister was it that at one moment I though *we* were the target, that they were about to attack *us*, the foreigners, the enemy.

I looked up at Gough and saw his face tense, eyes like slits on the spectacle as the leading men scorched past us to raptuous greeting from the inhabitants of Kitzbühel who seemed by now to have all turned out, thousands of arms raised in greeting. They were *welcoming* them! And here we were in the middle of the maelstrom; we the enemy of Germany, caught up in the invasion, a fanatic crowd pressing us from all sides and screaming their heads off for Hitler.

"Let's get the hell out of here," Gough said grimly. He proceeded to steer me through the ecstatic crowds. "That's Austria going, going, gone. Next Poland. With the Treaty we have then that's it." There was a certain excitement in his voice which terrified me. He was a soldier, trained to fight, and fight the black-clad menace he would with every ounce in him. With professional skill and steely determination he would fight them to the last drop of blood in his body.

Not everybody in Kitzbühel welcomed the Nazis. The manager of the Grand Hotel for one. He was as white as a sheet and wringing his hands in despair in the hallway when we appeared through the swing doors of the portals.

"Bloody Germans again," Geoffrey growled when we met him in the hall. "Just as well we're leaving tomorrow. First thing when I get home is to dig out my uniform."

"Leave the shooting to me this time Pa," Gough said, steel in his voice, and with it a knife in my heart.

I left the men talking to the distraught manager in the hall and went up to Babs in our room. "It's come to Austria," I said. "The Black Shirts are here and Kitzbühel is welcoming them with rapture."

"I wish they wouldn't make such a bloody noise about it," was all Babs said.

We left Austria just in time and with no illusions left as to what would happen next. The obscene sight of those black shirts swooping down on the nursery slopes of what had once been a 'little England', stayed imprinted on my mind, colouring everything I did until war was declared. In the forefront of Gough's thoughts was how to get through Babs' and Angus' wedding without sparking off an almighty row between the bridegroom and the father who, because of Angus' pacifist declaration, now openly showed their dislike of one another.

The family kindly said that I helped to diffuse the situation. I do not know, but on one occasion when the two men were about to have a confrontation in the middle of the wedding reception, I managed to steer Geoffrey away by saying I felt faint and needed a brandy. Concerned, he took me to the bar, and I was forced to gulp the stuff down neat so as not to give the game away. Later Gough teased me for being tiddly which I suppose I was having had unwanted brandy on top of all the champagne!

But the church ceremony went off smoothly. Babs looked magnificent in her tall statuesqueness. As for Angus, I definitely had a soft spot for him if one could ignore his political outbursts. In between he was like a cuddly teddy-bear: very braw and bonny in dress tartan which kilt clashed with his flaming head of hair.

After the church ceremony there was a guard of honour of Tank men in full dress uniform. Angus had been forced to bow to this military show on Babs' threat of breaking the whole thing off. The procession, led by bride and bridegroom trooped out from the church under an archway of shining swords with Gough one of the sword bearers. He looked particularly magnificent in this garb, and not just to me: there were plenty of admiring glances from girls and women whose eyes followed him wherever he went. His long legs were clad in dark blue tights that stretched over mirror polished mosquito boots; gold braid on shoulders, gold and blue belt with tassels on a tunic with black facings on the sleeves and stiff neckwear. His black beret was particularly proudly worn at the head of this smart outfit. The black berets, worn with just that extra élan with their shiny badges, never ceased to thrill me; Gough's of course in particular. It was something to do with the way his youthful springy hair showed above his left ear with the flap pulled well down on the right. He gave me a great wink as I passed under his sword.

I came down the church steps smiling broadly, and Dolly at my side, having seen the wink, was convulsed with giggles.

Chapter Ten

Knowing that the ideal life in Dorset could not last much longer now that it was high summer, I went down to Great Oaks Hall on every possible occasion whether Gough could get off work or not. Babs hardly ever came from Scotland. She was fully occupied in the restoration and refurbishing of their castle keep. From her phone calls she appeared to be supremely happy. She loved Scotland and she loved Angus!

Adele missed her daughter dreadfully and lapsed back into mourning. To Geoffrey's irritation she still wore black. When I chided her on her depressed outlook, she said she was mourning for Benjamin, for Babs and for the whole of Europe about to descend into an abyss. She would not listen to the news and walked out of the room if anyone turned the wireless on.

This annoyed Geoffrey all the more. I knew why. He was a man who believed one should face facts; he needed life and vigour around him; he needed sex. His need oozed through his skin. I could feel it, and he knew I could. If I had not been so in love with the family and so totally dedicated to Gough, I really think I would have been one of those in London to give him his need, such was the mature grey-haired man's magnetism. We had a sort of unspoken pact of fidelity between us. Even so, I made sure I was never in the Dolphin flat alone with him.

But Adele's spirits rose when Gough was posted for a few weeks to nearby Bovington, preparatory to joining the 2nd Royal Tank Regiment in Farnborough. Then we four threw care aside and enjoyed to the full every moment we had together. Gough introduced me to his friends at Bovington and asked them to Great Oaks Hall on every possible occasion. 'The boys of the black berets', I called them, and they called me 'Gough's girl'. We had a great deal of fun that summer, and we were acutely conscious of having fun, of snatching every minute of happiness with the future seen as a door, already creaking open, into a world of pain, suffering and partings.

Gough and I did not always seek to be alone. Mostly we went around in parties of young people. We played tennis or golf or swam in the fashionable Blue Pool or took picnics to the small cove by Lulworth where we changed behind rocks and braved, with tender-soled feet, the pebbly shore, and yelled exuberantly into the shock of the cold sea. I felt spoilt by the attention of all the surplus of men the Forces gave girls like myself. It boosted the low opinion I had had of myself until then to laughingly accept their compliments, while all the time I basked in the love Gough lavished on me.

Often we went sailing. The Nicholsons kept a boat in Poole Harbour. Geoffrey, Adele and I went on our own when Gough could not get away. Then Adele, in grey trousers and light coloured aertex shirt, seemed happiest. The wind whipped up the

111

colour into her cheeks and made her eyes sparkle until Geoffrey declared she looked again like the girl he had married.

We would take a hamper bulging with salads and cold game pie prepared in the kitchens of the Hall; fresh lemonade for us ladies to quench our thirst on hot days, beer for Geoffrey. We sailed away from the quay by the picturesque white-washed houses with their gabled roofs, and tacked hither and thither in the wide harbour beyond where the ferry ran, until I too became quite expert at navigating, going about without crashing my head on the boom and even taking sails down and putting up the jib.

For lunch we sailed up creeks and chose a spot to disembark; and we talked endlessly of the 'children' – the three children – and how they loved anything to do with the water; rowing, small boat sailing, swimming . . .

I remember one day in particular when we all four had been sailing. After we had tied up to the quay, Geoffrey helped his wife ashore and stood with her there, arms around her little figure. Gough took my hand.

"It's lovely to see them like that," he remarked. "They do love one another very much, as I love you."

"Why do you love me?" I asked, my happiness spilling over, "I'm just a very ordinary girl."

"I need you more than you know," he said squeezing my hand so hard it hurt. "You're staunch and loyal and I need to know you are there thinking and praying for me in this bloody war that's coming. Sometimes I'm afraid of the responsibility, afraid I may let my men down, afraid I won't come up to scratch in a crisis."

"I have no doubts on that score, Gough," I replied, hiding my feelings at the thought of him in the thick of it with his men.

"It is a relief to share one's anxieties. I have never, and never will, let on to anyone else. You'd come if I wanted you?"

"Of course . . . to the ends of the earth." I did not say, 'to some grizzly field hospital' which picture immediately sprang to my mind.

One of the times I remember with great clarity during that last summer of peace, was being invited to Bovington for the Open Day. In a group of excited small boys I was shown the inside of a tank with its clutter of living necessities, of blankets and folded greatcoats, camouflage nets, tarpaulins, unditching tools (Gough said tanks were always being ditched) chains, ropes and spares. Perhaps most vital of all was the cooking stove with which to brew up a restoring mug of tea after a long hard days work.

"A tight fit for you," I looked up at the six foot plus form of Gough peering down at me. "I don't know how you find the space to curl up in here!"

"I manage," he replied with a grin.

I loved seeing him in uniform. He had taken me to lunch in the Mess. I thought him very fine in his dress khaki, khaki shirt and tie, shining belt over tunic, tank badge on lapels, red shoulder straps for 'A' battalion, powerful chest bare of medals, a worsted badge of a Mark I worn on his right arm.

"What is the badge for?" I asked as I sat beside him in the Mess for lunch where the room was very fine too, with a highly polished table laid with immaculate silver, the officers and their guests waited on as if we were royalty. "The badge reminds me of my days in the Girl Guides!"

"I'll have you know it is as good as any medal," Gough snorted. "Awarded to officers and men alike once they have passed the exacting test of membership of a tank crew."

"A test which shows one is capable of repairing any old Rolls Royce engine," I laughed.

After lunch we stood outside looking up at the brown, red, and green regimental colours straining from the flag-pole in a stiff breeze from the sea. Wind, strong winds, were the norm at Bovington.

"It dates from the Battle of Cambrai in 1917 where very many lost their lives," Gough informed. "General Elles led the Tank Corps into battle that day. The colours signify from mud through blood to the green fields beyond."

I looked up wordlessly at Gough. His glance caught mine. Gough with all the other enthusiastic men of that generation knew what they were in for. "The green fields beyond," I repeated softly. "We only have to survive to reach them."

"God willing, we will," Gough said.

On another occasion, I was down at Great Oaks alone with Adele. We were walking back to the car after having visited one of her retired tenants in the nearby picturesque village of Longbride. All was quiet and peaceful in this most lovely part of southern Dorset, when a slight rumble was heard on the still, hot, air.

"What's that? Thunder?" asked Adele cocking an ear to listen. The sound grew louder.

"Unmistakable," I said with my new-found knowledge, "it can only be the clatter of caterpillar tracks on Tarmacadamed road."

We stood together on the verge of the village's small green, by a cross-road with signpost, to watch them pass. They were led by a flat-nosed Morris with canvas top, a white flag attached to the side wing. Then the first tank came lumbering into view followed by a stream of others as far as we could see along the straightness of the stretch of road.

As the first vehicle neared I noticed the number on the right lower front of the tank: MK 8360. The armament looked formidable with its two menacing machine-guns pointing forwards at us. Above the number and inside the armament peered the face of the driver, headphones on. Over him, and on the same side, perched two youthful looking crew both with gas mask bags slung round their chests and one wearing muddy wellington boots. Behind them again, and way above in the turret, stood an officer. He too was wearing headphones and could be seen talking into his mouthpiece as they neared the cross-roads where we stood. The officer wore goggles pushed up over his beret. Behind him a thin aerial with pennant, stuck up into the air and waved wand-like in the wind stream. On the platform before the officer lay a clutter of maps clipped to boards, binoculars, compass markers and other instruments.

Simultaneously, and with broad smiles, Adele and I clutched at one another. It *had* to be Gough! It *was* Gough! It was predestined. We did not expect him to recognize the figures of two women on the green watching, what with the noise the long convoy made and his concentration on his job in the leading of it.

115

He was 'on duty'. A stranger to us, intent on his work with no thought for the women in his life.

Adele and I stood on, mesmerized by the sight and unable to talk through the noise. But as the tank started to round the corner, Gough saw us, and grinned his familiar grin. Giving us a cheery wave, in seconds he had passed by on his way.

We were left exalted and stood rooted on the grass like star-struck movie fans. The rest of the convoy rumbled past while we waved exuberantly to the men led by *our* Gough; men, wonderful men who rode these hideous, grim, grey monsters of iron, the vehicles' interiors packed with engines, pipes, instruments, fuel tanks, ammunition for the big guns and the machine guns, food and water rations for the crews. The mammoths were faceless, noisy, smelly and menacing – and these were not even heavy tanks.

I had seen such tanks parked at Bovington, been inside the one on the open public day and found its inside claustrophobic in the extreme, a death trap – a fire trap. Gough had told me how in battle the driver would have his visor down and would drive blind by the exact instructions given over the intercom, to turn for this degree to left or right or reverse, instructions given by his captain in the revolving turret who held all their lives in his hands.

Now I had seen the captain in his towering turret giving his orders, seen *Gough* giving his instructions, and I found that the flesh and blood fact of the personality of the leader gave the whole exercise a flair as of cavalry of old, gave a certain magnificence with a splendour all of its own. In my imagination I saw it as a coloured moving picture of the life Gough was leading and was going to lead into battle. It was noisy; it spewed obnoxious fumes; it was monstrous – and it was magnificent!

Taken from my 1939 'Line a day' diaries:

August 21
Haven't heard from Gough since I last saw him riding past in his tank at Longbride. *Always* manoeuvres. News very grave. Russia joining forces with enemy Germany. How *can* they? England is stunned by this betrayal.

August 24
International situation worse than ever. I haven't been able to get down at weekends but Adele tells me Geoffrey is busy arming the estate to the teeth in preparation for the Germans, even to taking spears and lances off the walls of the old armoury! In lieu of his last war service he has been told he'll be called up to the War Office. Nowhere near my department, but I shall be seeing him around to exchange family news. Adele said the Dorset coast is now heavily armed; roads leading to Bovington are barred off, armed vehicles met everywhere. Gough wrote to say I *must* put a telephone into the flat or he will lose me. If Germany walks into Poland, as seems extremely likely any minute, there will be war, and with Russia against us how can we hope to win? The thought of those Black Shirts we saw in Kitzbühel ruling us in Parliament does not bear thinking of. Babs wrote that she would shoot herself rather than be under the Nazis, but

Angus is going to welcome the Communists in!
Babs is expecting a baby.

August 25

President Roosevelt has appealed to Germany, Italy and Poland for peace. Reservists called up. Denys, whom I first met in that pea souper, is one of them. He came to see me in the flat. Such a dear. He's off to France. Those days when he and John were my boyfriends are a world away. Both know about Gough and wish us well. John is posted with his unit from India to Iraq where it is 'bloody hot'!

August 26

In this fog of uncertainty that surrounds us, rumours abound at the War Office. The latest one is that Germany has marched into Danzig.

August 27

Crisis the same; concentration of German forces on Polish front. More and more troops moving up all the time. I do not see how war can be averted. My work is now classed 'highly secret'. (As if it wasn't before!) Under Mr Williams. Changed to M12 Signal 6 on Typex side. We are non-persons. Incognito civilians. People ask me why I am not in uniform. I say I make the tea! Gough dashed into the flat. Furious with me that I have not yet had a telephone put in. 'Will do, sir,' I saluted. He is enormously fit and all buoyed up raring to go. War OK for him in his tank, says I; what about the women and children sitting ducks in

London? We went dancing at the Hammersmith Palais. Danced for hours expending a great deal of surplus energy. Best jazz bands in the world there. Then fondling in the flat. Went further than we ever have before. Gough is always the one to bring us back to the straight and narrow.

August 28
Played 18 holes of golf with Gough and his father at Great Oaks Hall and then two sets of tennis in p.m. The only answer to this continuing anxiety is to exhaust oneself physically. Even so could not sleep so read Mary Webb's *Seven for a Secret* in my Rose room half the night. Apparently Gough has no trouble sleeping!

August 29
On the brink of war. Everyone ready for it to begin at any moment. That's the beginning, but what of the end? Will any of my beloved adopted family be here to see it – Gough, Geoffrey, Adele, Babs, Angus? If Gough is killed I hope I am too. The days and nights drag out, waiting for war.

August 30
Situation slightly better. Germany suggests making a pact with Great Britain. What *is* Hitler up to? Does he *really* think we would renege and break our treaty with Poland? If he thinks so he had better think again! Hours on my phone to Gough.

September 1

Germany has invaded Poland and bombed some towns. So tomorrow, or even tonight, we will be at war. God knows how or when it will end.

September 2

Germany bombed Warsaw. Why we are not retaliating I do not know. Spoke to Gough over the phone. He does not know either!

September 3

Great Britain and France declared war on Germany at 11 a.m. when the ultimatum was up. No news of fighting on the ground or whether our Air Force has attacked yet. Chamberlain made a great speech but he sounded tired out. Poor man, all his efforts for peace have come to nothing.

Chapter Eleven

Life went on. Apart from the unfamiliar yowl of an air raid warning whilst I was at work, when, with dry mouths, we girls collected our gas masks kept to hand and descended with our files into the basement, routine went on much as usual. On the first occasion of the alarm nothing happened and in a short time we were back at our desks. No one seemed to know whether it was a false alarm or whether those in charge were just trying the sirens out. It caused a good deal of confusion, but was helpful as a rehearsal for things to come; and come they did when, later, we worked permanently in the basement only coming up at lunch time to view the light of day.

Altogether the 'phoney war' was a strange sort of time to be working in London. We were at war, yet not at war. This non-war virtually went on until May of the following year. The only war news that I, at any rate, could talk about were reports from the newspapers of boats attacked at sea as early as September 4th when the German navy torpedoed a passenger ship off the Hebrides with three hundred Americans on board. Most people believed that would bring the United States into the war. It did not.

More isolation and bitterness was felt when South Africa 'ratted' and declared themselves neutral. To us in the UK it seemed a betrayal of kith and kin, though Hertzog had the decency to resign in protest. We read of merchant ships sunk in home waters. The RAF did not help much. They bombed the Kiel Canal without, apparently, any great success, but with the loss of five of our planes and their crews. It was all very depressing and frustrating.

The most frustrated man of all was Gough when the British Expeditionary Force under General Gort began its cross-channel move to join the French armies. The BEF landed at Cherbourg. By the time the 1st Armoured Corps moved forward to the frontier, the Polish Army had collapsed.

Why Gough was nearly mad with frustration was because he was now stationed in Farnborough, had been promoted to temporary rank of Captain, and made Adjutant of the 2nd Royal Tank Regiment. But *they* were not going to the Front! They were equipped with Mark I tanks such as I had seen driving through the village of Longbride. Mark IIs were needed to combat the larger German tanks. Some cavalry units, including the 12th Lancers, schooled in the handling of armoured cars, had been brought up to strength on mobilization, and, together with a great many reservists, were amongst those embarking.

Gough was still fuming at this 'injustice' when we met in the lunch hour at Lyon's Corner House in Piccadilly. I was already seated at a small table when he walked in looking marvellous as always in uniform, new pips up. He bent to give me a smacking kiss on the lips.

"Well . . .?" I said as he sat down in his usual slouching position, long legs stretched out before him. "What are you up here for?"

"A meeting about the rushed production of Mark IIs. That's what's delayed our departure. Bloody inefficient."

"Good," I said. "Thank God you haven't gone dashing off to war in your little Mark Is to be slaughtered by the great Panzer Model F. Tank."

"How do you know that?" he asked suspiciously. The waitress came up and we ordered sausages and mash.

"It comes my way through code scrambling," I declared airily. "Most of it goes into my unconscious, but I wake up when tanks are mentioned having taken a personal interest in them."

"Then you can tell me why the 4th RTR were sent off from Farnborough when they too have only got Mark Is?"

"I guess you are too valuable in reserve," I replied flippantly. "I for one am as pleased as Punch you *haven't* gone!"

"The Russians have entered Poland. Are they allies or not? Nobody knows. According to all accounts the French are fighting magnificently; poor Frogs attacked all over again twenty years after the last clash. Not so good with the Royal Navy. Did you hear that *HMS Courageous* has been sunk in the North Sea? And all the RAF do is to drop pamphlets on the Germans. A blind bit of use that is. What's the matter with everyone?"

"You *are* gloomy," I observed while watching him tuck into his plateful. I started on mine.

"What do you expect? Of course I am gloomy sitting there in Farnborough waiting for equipment which hasn't yet been *made*. When at last we do get it we'll have to do a heck of a lot more training before they'll let us go. 'Aha,' he sighed, with a chuckle at me. "'How dull it is to rust unburnished, not to shine in use.' Bet you don't know who wrote that?"

"Bad luck. Bet I do. Alfred Lord Tennyson. Have you seen your parents this time?"

"Not yet. Shall be there tonight. Have you?"

"I've heard from your mother about the installing of East End children at Great Oaks."

"That's right. I'm happy to say the war seems to have given her a new lease of life. She says she plans to leave the kids in the charge of the housekeeper and our old nanny and come and live in the flat with Pa and do some of yours and Babs' Isle of Dogs canteen work."

"Splendid! We badly need volunteers, so many have been called up. Dolly's joined the ATS."

We scraped our plates and ordered coffee. "You know, darling," said Gough thoughtfully while counting out the luncheon money on the table, "I don't think you are going to make a very good army wife if you are against your husband going to war to do what he's been trained up to the eyeballs to do," he teased. It was the first time he had mentioned 'wife' and I glowed at the word. Friends all round were rushing off to get married at Caxton Hall. Not so Gough who rigidly stuck to his policy of 'not before I'm on the strength' and anyway what was the good of marrying in wartime? Better to wait until it was all over and have a proper white wedding as Babs had.

Underlying his reluctance, I knew of course, was his passion for his Corps and his fear that domesticity and family responsibility would erode it and dilute his drive and fervour. It seemed to me that in his bones he knew that when eventually he married, he would

124

want to put his wife and family first. I had seen him at Bovington Open Day showing the children round the tanks. He would make a marvellous father, especially to a son. This I understood and accepted without too much difficulty. I felt an older man would have been ready for marriage, but Gough for all the appearance he gave of strength and leadership, was trying his wings still. He was only two years older than I and with a brilliant career before him. If I wanted Gough I would have to wait for him. At times I wondered how it was that this man so dedicated to his work loved me at all.

But it was after that rushed lunch meeting that I began to recognize that his still-young age and dedication to his career was not the whole story. Were they excuses? That he loved me I had no doubt, but I now glimpsed that there was something more in the depth of this extraordinarily attractive personality that was hidden to me and maybe even hidden to him; something that perhaps I would one day have to acknowledge, to fully understand the nature of the man I loved unreservedly while he appeared to hold back. One day I would find out . . .

I am not going to recount in detail from my diary what I did during the long months of the 'phoney war' for there is little to recount. Life went on much the same. There were no particular shortages of food or goods. Women were called up in greater numbers, many going into munition factory work, or to the country as land girls. My work kept me excessively busy with long hours, often into the night, with little time or inclination for recreation.

The Isle of Dogs went out of the window for me.

But I heard about it from Adele who had taken wholeheartedly to her 'war work', every now and then dashing down to Great Oaks Hall to check up on the growing staff needed to look after the dozens of children there in what had become a boarding school. To my gratification Adele and Geoffrey seemed happier in their eyrie in London than I had ever seen them. The war had given them purpose and rejuvenated them. War had advantages to some.

Gough and I met whenever we could which was not often. I waited for him to ring me at home – he had given me strict instructions never to ring him in the Mess unless it was a real emergency. At Christmas I joined the family in the roomy top flat of Osborne House in Dolphin Square with its beautiful views of the river, particularly attractive at night. Babs and Angus did not come down; too busy cultivating the land for vegetables. We gathered growing 'tatties' was allowed as reserve occupation.

It was a cosy, happy Christmas for the four of us. Geoffrey always made me laugh. It was the way he said it rather than what he said. He had a lovely sense of humour which he had passed on to his son. Before we retired to our rooms at night Adele brewed her night cap of milky Horlicks. Geoffrey usually managed to surreptitiously pour his down the lavatory to my amusement when stealthily he returned from pulling the plug. Gough drank his up like a man. Mostly we had our meals in the downstairs restaurant, once in the West End after a theatre. We all went back to work after Boxing Day.

Gough quickly got over his disappointment at not going to France with the initial British Expeditionary Force. He was kept too busy to think of much other

126

than the business in hand. Adjutants of a Regiment had an exacting often onerous, though rewarding, job. Gough was his CO's right-hand man required to know everything going on in the squadron and report on it. Particularly he watched over the men's needs and sorted out problems with families. He was ideally suited for this. But first he was a fighting man and the training with the new armoured fighting vehicles (known as the AFV's) was all important when the tanks began to be delivered straight off the factory lines.

The training was extensive and exhaustive; they were kept at it night and day. There was always more training to be done, for every conceivable circumstance had to be, if possible, forseen and prepared for. The exacting CO of the 2nd RTR made certain that all his officers passed on to the men every little intricacy of the immensely complicated rumbling monsters they were manoeuvering. With their hundreds of thousands of separate parts, tanks were vilely accident prone. It was vital that any deficiency or fault that had missed the initial tests must be found out and corrected in the workshops before going to the Front.

As Gough once said to me: "A tank is no bloody use if it breaks down when facing enemy guns. In that stranded situation they are worse than useless, positively dangerous sitting targets of sealed infernos. Things are always going wrong with these brand new vehicles. Faulty castings are found. Arms break off. Tracks get bogged down on sandy beaches. Oh, my God, what a shenanigan!"

Gough never divulged where he went when he disappeared for days and weeks at a time on these extensive manoeuvres, but it was well known in the land that the whole of the south coast of England was one huge training area made to resemble the landscape of northern Europe, and thick with defensive devices.

The same phoney lull that we had at home was going on in Europe during which time the Germans raised their strength on the Western Front to crack troops said to be the equal of 136 divisions. Polish forces were converted with new armaments into Panzer fighting units. The French too raised more divisions which together with the Belgians and Dutch as well as the British already there, gave the allies superiority in numbers. The hectic rearmament during the 'lull' augured well for the allies.

Gough rang: "I'm back in Farnborough. There's a jolly on at the Aldershot Officer's Club the day after tomorrow. The idea is that social engagements carry on as norm, even if the Hun starts to bomb us. Can you drop everything and come?"

"Rather!" I had been to those club dances before with the tank boys. They were the greatest fun, ending at 4 am with breakfast as they had at Sandhurst.

All my times with Gough were magical, but this dance at the end of April 1940 had a special wonder about it. We both knew it would be our last dance for a long time.

"You look marvellous," he said. I was ridiculously happy to see Gough again, bronzed and sinewy fit and altogether gorgeous. As always I was intoxicated by his masculinity. Glimpsing myself in the long door mirror in the club's entrance lobby, I saw myself rosy with happiness, eyes bright and reflecting the sea-green of my long, softly-pleated dress. If I looked 'marvellous' it was only because of Gough.

The precincts of the Aldershot Club were in reality rather drab, but to me that night it was a palace with its sprung parquet floor that bounced with every step and must have made even the heaviest of females feel as light as a feather. Dancing a quick fox-trot with Gough I felt as if I was taking off on wings. The clubhouse, built in the last century, looked like a whitened Indian bungalow with a tiled roof. The ballroom contained the most of it, a large room with regimental badges lining the walls. Glass doors reflected the inevitable army green paint as a background to the dancing throng. High up were clear-storey windows. In a gallery at the back sat some of the more senior members framed by a portrait of King George VI. Off the ballroom were roomy lounges in which to sit, and down the corridors were several bars and buffets.

It was our night. Though we knew many others at the club we danced only together, bodies closer as the evening drew on. There was excitement and sensuousness in our dancing. We were young, in love. We were beautiful in ourselves . . . heads together, dreamy, eyes only for one another. Even on a dance floor Gough was the quintessential professional soldier head and shoulders above the rest. When we moved to one or another of the lounges for the buffet, or just to sit in the leather chairs, I could see envy in the other girls' eyes. He was mine exclusively that night and I was queen of the ball!

We went out into the evening and wandered arm in arm round the red tennis courts; we stood by the pool and watched the antics of hardy bathers taking a dip with shouts as they plunged in under the cold gaze of a full moon. We were imbued with happiness; so good to be alive; our bodies supple and straight, our heads held high, our lips smiling, ourselves unafraid – for how could we be afraid when we were together?

"I'll remember this night for ever," Gough said as, hungry, we partook of breakfast.

"I too," I said wiping my chin and tucking my starched napkin more firmly into my low-cut dress so that my cleft showed.

"You have the sweetest little bosoms," Gough observed.

He drove me back to London. I slept all the way, my head on his shoulder. He took me up the stairs and saw me safely into the flat.

"Whatever happens in future doesn't matter, darling," he said. "What matters is that we've had all this. *Grace de Dieu* we were given a second chance and we took it with both hands."

"What would you have done if we had not met again?"

"I'd have become a cynical old bachelor," he grinned. He kissed me, waved, and drove off back to Farnborough in the dawn in time to start a full days work. No sleep for him that night. It was more good training for what was to come.

On the 7th of May there was a phone call from Adele. Gough was coming up; could I stay? I could not but I was able to leave the office for a few hours to be with him and his parents in Dolphin Square. Though nothing was said we all knew this must be his embarkation leave.

130

There were no tears; the fears Geoffrey, Adele and I felt were suppressed. Gough did not try and hide his excitement and thrill to at last be going into action, and we were proud of him. He was going off to do what he had been trained to do and he would do it brilliantly.

On May 10th of that fateful year of 1940 the Germans struck. The British Expeditionary Force rushed into Belgium and into the fray. It did not augur well for the allies.

Gough rang me 'from somewhere' before he took off for the Continent. I cannot remember what he said or what I said. I just listened to the voice I loved so much. The silence that ensued seemed deafening in the empty void that his departure left.

Part Three

Chapter Twelve

It felt as if a lifetime had passed before the first letter came.

29/5/40
Darling,
   At last a moment to drop you a line. Since we left at an hour's notice on 22nd we have been in almost continuous action. Haven't had a moment to rest or think. I've snatched short sleep in the most extraordinary positions including standing up! I reckon an average of 1½ hours a day for 6 days is no fun.
   After a long day and night sprint across France, we went straight into action, the first time for most. I can tell you it frightened all of us quite a bit! I lost some good friends; far the worst part. Looking forward very much to a change of socks and shirt. You would not like me at all let alone recognize me. The foul weather hasn't helped either. I got so soaked one night that I had to wear my sweater under my shirt and still catch forty winks sleep in a puddle. But one gets used to it.
   I've experienced most sorts of unpleasantness from dive-bombing to machine gun fire, shells

and mortar bombs. Men quite marvellous. They manage to brew something up to keep us officers awake and going even in a five minute lull. We've passed from one world of the green fields in a pleasant land to a vile bloodstained one in which we kill and get killed against all decent instincts. There is, though, thrill in destroying the enemy's marathon monsters and then getting the hell out of it.

We are being issued with Field postcards so will send one to the parents asking for English newspapers, chocolates, and cigarettes. No time at present for any more and anyway no means of carrying them. I am as homesick as when I was a small prep school boy for news of home and family, but I am very fit though tired and dirty. Hope you got the car safely and are enjoying driving it. See how I trust you with my most precious possession!

All my love, your Gough.
3/6/40

Dearest one,
Marvellous to get your letter and parcel of goodies plus the telephone message from Pa from the War Office with news of rewards and praise for the Royal Tank boys which has encouraged all on the ground very much. We are here to rest and refit, and are quite close to a place where a certain French lady of warlike spirit was bumped off by an English king in days of yore. You can guess! Very pleasant and restful it is too after the exertions of the last ten days. No one knows quite

how long we are likely to be so peaceful. I have at last had the chance of a bath – not a real one, but a wash by sections. We are at present in quite a large *château*; only no electricity, no water and no sanitary arrangements! To add to our difficulties one of our soldiers has just dropped the chain and bucket down the local well. As it is about 50 feet down to water level, and in there about 30 feet deep, conditions have not improved. Lovely countryside. Unbelievable with the war raging no distance away. I look out onto a blissful scene of apple orchards and cows grazing.

Last night I had my first good night's rest since setting out twelve days previously. About 11 hours hogging it. Good it was. But oh! for a pint of English beer and a water closet!

Some orders have come in and I must get on with dealing with them. Best of luck to everyone at home.

All my love darling.
Your Gough.

PS. Had a letter from Babs. They are up to their eyes in land work. I hope she doesn't overdo it now they have the wee bairn. But you know what Babs is, the strapping girl!

Those two letters were the only ones I received from Gough on the European Front. I already knew a good deal more about it than most people through my top secret work at the War Office. Later I was able to piece together the short and devastating campaign which won Gough his first "gong". The citation read:

'For conspicuous gallantry and outstanding leadership carried out with unquenchable cheerfulness and inspiration to his men'.

Later still, when I researched in great depths Gough's military career I discovered that his reference to 'leaving at an hour's notice on 22nd May' meant that two Royal Tank Regiments left Farnborough to embark at Dover where their guns were packed about in mineral jelly to protect them from the salt water on the crossing. They landed without mishap at Cherbourg on May 23 and made straight for the tank training area at Pacy, south of the Seine. They reached it covered in grease from their guns.

Given no time to clean up they were told to move immediately to the west of Amiens from where they were to advance to the Somme to relieve the pressure on the BEF, now in dire danger of being cut off by the enemy.

Already tired and filthy dirty, Gough and his men reached the Somme the next day after an eerie black-out seventy-five mile drive on a very dark night in heavy rain and damp mist. Driving without lights it was almost impossible to pick out the tiny pin point of the tail light of the vehicle ahead. They were fired on, met road blocks, and got lost. Vehicles broke down; others had to be left stranded in ditches. They were short of every sort of equipment including telescopes, wirelesses and ammunition. Even so they managed to rendezvous successfully with the Brigade.

They were ordered to press on, through open rolling country sprinkled with small woods and valleys, to reach the Somme in one bound. Once there they found themselves shut out from the main body of the

BEF by the motorized divisions of the Germans. They ran into heavy mortar fire, and Gough's squadron was badly shot up in his first baptism of fire. They reassembled with the 3rd Armoured Brigade, but found they were unable to make further progress.

The Brigade was now put under French command whose motorized cavalry had had a shattering encounter with the Germans in the Ardennes, and in consequence had failed to arrive in time to back up the British tanks. In the *impasse* Gough was ordered to take a patrol and probe the enemy's defences. This he did in a wooded area where he ran head-on into the most enormous tank he had ever seen. As he later admitted, he was scared stiff by its very size! Nevertheless he managed to open fire first. His gun, in comparison to the German one, looked like a pea-shooter. To his surprise the attack debilitated the tank enough for him to take the crew prisoner.

After this first shock encounter to give him a taste of things to come, Gough carried on with his patrol and successfully penetrated through enemy lines as far north as Boisemont near the estuary of the Somme. From there he brought back valuable information on enemy dispersements.

It was in the ensuing lull after reporting back that Gough found time to pen his first letter. A few days later he wrote the second 'rest and refit' one with the hint that he was near Rouen. But he was not left long in the château. By June 5 they were back on the Somme waiting for the next enemy strike. It soon came.

Having finished their round-up to the north, the German Panzers switched southwards and eastwards, and, with a rapidity of mechanized mobility which was to leave the allies gasping, attacked in a pincer-movement.

On June 8 Rommel began his thrust to Rouen, by-passing the main roads (where the opposition was hiding in strategically placed road blocks) to avoid the enemy.

On that same evening, Gough and his squadron were the last to leave Andelys. In a brilliant and desperate rearguard action to hold off the German forces and enable the remains of the Division to get across the Seine, his squadron destroyed a number of better and more heavily equipped tanks thus gaining valuable time for the bulk to beat the retreat.

At one point, and in the middle of a raging battle, Gough led his tank on foot back into the foray. He personally picked up and carried to his tank men he had seen lying wounded beside their incapacitated vehicles. It was for this personal bravery and his magnificent leadership in the next few days, when coolly he hung on and covered the withdrawal of others, that Gough was awarded the Military Cross.

With the whole Front now in collapse the orders were to withdraw and follow the French division due southwards in an endeavour to cross the Seine before it was too late. This, by hook and by crook, they did, crossing the river by Andelys which town was on fire, a spectacular and awe-inspiring sight for the tank commanders watching from their turrets.

For Gough, after the Seine crossing in which the waters reflected the conflagration, came days and nights of endless driving on unknown and congested roads. Tanks peeled off having run out of fuel, others broke down. The tanks that went on were packed with stranded soldiers. The men were in a bemusement from lack of knowledge of what was going on and what had gone wrong, but knowing that this was a defeat of the direst proportions. To the officers particularly the depressing knowledge was compounded by enormous tiredness as day followed night and night followed day on the road.

The days and nights seemed unending as Gough stood in his turret with aching feet, his body bruised all over from the jolting on cobbled streets and uneven roads. Smoke from burning houses hindered visibility; bodies of old men, women and children lay on the roadsides, on the verges and in the ditches. The stink of war was in his nostrils. His eyes, bleary from fatigue, took in the horrors of a country overrun by enemy.

Through the black nights, Gough forced himself to keep awake enough behind the French division not to crash into the vehicle ahead. And all the time was the fighting off of exhaustion, the lack of food, and the worry of the 'fog of war' with not knowing what was going on to the north where the guns could be heard blasting off, so close was the enemy to them. Were the allies putting up a substantial fight against the Germans over there? If so why could not they go to relieve them in their turn, or was it that resistance had turned into a rout?

All Gough knew at that stage was that the French division was immediately ahead of him on the road and that he had orders to follow it, but he knew only too well the depth of his personal sorrow at the men he had lost, and felt the gut-horror of the huge disaster in which he was partaking. He knew that his fighting force had been decimated and that all that remained of the 3rd Armoured Brigade after seven days of fighting was two weak squadrons – his and another RTR – with some light tanks gathered in from other units.

At Alençon the men in the reduced British force were at last able to snatch some sleep. A count was made. The Brigade by now consisted of only four hundred and nine officers and men, twenty-nine tanks and sixty vehicles with enough scrounged petrol to, hopefully, cover the two hundred and twenty-five miles still to go. They pressed on. At one point where they turned due north from their westwards course towards St Lo, they actually crossed Rommel's route a bare few hours ahead of the enemy. At St Lo they heard that the French were sueing for peace terms.

Due to a bridge reported down to the north, the column diverted westwards towards the coast at Lessey, a route on which they had to slow right down to force their way through the heavily congested roads of fleeing populace. In the midst of this bedlam, Gough drove on, his tank sniped at and filthy, but mercifully still running. Breakdowns had to be left behind leaving men to work frantically on them in an effort to repair the vehicles in time to catch up. The fitter lorries and their plucky crews brought up the rear of the convoy. Those that did not make it were captured and became prisoners of war for up to five years. In the final day, Gough drove one hundred and seventy-five miles in twenty hours. Overall he had covered four hundred miles in six days and nights.

And on June 17, he with the others at last saw the sea at Cherbourg ahead of Rommel's forces now racing almost parallel to them to the west. All Gough's brand new fourteen tanks arrived on the dockside intact, and of his light tanks only two failed to turn up.

Though travel-stained and weary, Gough and his crew were elated to have got their tanks back to Cherbourg before Rommel could cut them off from the port. The highest credit was given to the Brigade for their feat of saving the precious tanks for another day.

Though at the time Gough did not know it, it had been a desperately close run. In his final dash due north to Cherbourg in the dark of the night, Rommel had been only a few hours behind their column. It turned out that at midnight the Germans had met with some artillery fire, and, unable in the dark to gauge the extent of the resistance, Rommel had decided to wait until daybreak lest they run into an ambush. After all, Rommel was later to write, he felt they had done pretty well to advance one hundred and fifty miles through enemy territory! But he was soon not so sanguine about having stopped for the rest of the night. On June 18, and after some resistance from the forts in the port, when Rommel looked down on the harbour he found it empty of ships. He had achieved a great and momentous victory, but to his way of thinking too many British had escaped over their narrow channel.

Though Gough was more than fortunate to have come through the *blitzkrieg* alive, unwounded and without having been taken prisoner, the defeat through France had been a bitter and salutory experience, an experience which left its mark. He had done all that was asked of him and more and he had come home to receive the Military Cross, but there

143

was no rejoicing. If before he had been youthfully enthusiastic to get at the enemy and do his bit for England, now he was grimly determined to reverse the rout with no illusions left as to what that would entail. Certainly there was no glory in it. War was a dirty, exhausting, bestial, messy business which killed and maimed. The only redeeming features to him were his 'bloody marvellous' men, and the birth of his interest in strategy.

He was left with a steely resolve to have another go at the Hun and this time beat him good and proper by superior tactics.

And in the process of his baptism of fire, Gough learnt a great deal about himself. He learnt that under the fiercest of attacks he could swallow the fear that lurked under the cool brow. He found that his brain stayed steel cold, calculating and exact at what was needed to be done and how best to do it in the heat of battle. He saw when to retreat, round, and come in again at the enemy's most vulnerable point. He could see at a quick glance a chance opening up, and in seconds was ordering the manoeuvering into position of his tanks through the intercom.

That those under Gough had faith in and believed in his judgement with an intrinsic love and trust there was no doubt. They would follow him blind from the bowels of the tank which had become their home, and they would give their lives to save him from wounding, death or capture.

The senior officers noted that he was a leader in the best tradition of the Corps. At the next vacancy he would be promoted.

Gough Nicholson, the soldier, was on his way . . .

Chapter Thirteen

Exactly four weeks from the day he left, Gough was back in this country. It was on June 19 that he rang me in the evening, and with blessed relief I heard his voice again.

"How are you?" I asked formally because I could think of nothing else to say.

"Fine, but dog tired. I'll tell you about it sometime."

"You weren't wounded, or, or, anything . . .?"

"Not even a graze," he laughed.

"When can I see you?"

"No proper leave as such. Too much to do. But I'm taking next weekend off with the parents in London. Bring the car and stay. They're expecting you. Babs is coming down."

"I'll miss the car," I said with truth. It was a lovely car to drive. I had learnt to drive it in two lessons flat round Holland Park and after that was away in the London traffic. It gave me a heady feeling of freedom after all the years of public transport.

"You'll be having it again any minute."

"Oh *no*! So soon . . ." My voice trailed away.

"There's been a bloody awful defeat and the sooner we get to grips with putting that right the better.

God . . . I'm nodding off . . . asleep on my feet. So long, darling . . ." he rang off.

The news of Gough's MC preceded him, and letters of congratulation arrived at the flat before he did. Babs had left the infant heir behind in Scotland with Angus and nanny. She looked weather-beaten. I gathered she spent all day out in the fields hoeing up potatoes. Gough had not yet arrived.

"Just listen to this one from Cousin Jack," Adele positively purred. She read aloud: "'I hear Gough has been awarded the MC. Splendid! You must be a *very* proud mother!' My goodness, I certainly am, and oh, this one from Durnford, the headmaster of his old prep school: 'We are bursting with pride and excitement here about Gough's award. We must get him over to talk to the boys some time. He's a hero! I have always had the highest possible opinion of him since he was a small boy, and now his bravery has been recognized.'"

We heard the clash of the lift outside and rushed to open the flat door to Gough before he had time to ring. He kissed and hugged us all. Adele dissolved into tears, and he held her tight for a moment. He looked the same yet not the same. He was a good bit leaner, and when his face was in repose, after that first exuberant moment, the strain he had been through showed.

To his mother's anxious enquiries he gave the same answer: "I've had a couple of night's sleep but I need more, and oh, Ma, lots of lovely grub. I can tell you I now know what it is like to starve!"

We all clattered down to the restaurant talking excitedly. Geoffrey joined us there. He was in uniform, Great War medals on his broad chest. He was working some distance away from me in another department of the War Office, but occasionally we would meet hurrying along in a corridor of the lofty building. Father and son kissed, Geoffrey slapping him on the back. I liked to see that. Geoffrey always kissed me on meeting, nuzzling in a little.

"Doesn't sound as if 'On Active Service' army rations are any better than they were in the last do, old man," Geoffrey growled.

"We existed on brew-ups and hard biscuits, Pa, as I expect you did. The whole performance was a bloody walk over from start to finish as far as I could see. One brigade arrived on French soil as we were pulling out and never fired a shot. Bet they lost a hell of a lot of equipment. It was a *blitzkrieg* all right. Our guns and armaments couldn't compete with the enemy's. Our tanks need thicker armour. Far too thin-skinned at present. We need 40 to 80mm armour. And bigger guns. Two pounders are hardly adequate."

"Don't gulp your food," reproved his mother. "You'll get tummy-ache."

Gough grinned and turned to his sister. "Where's my nephew? I'm longing to tell him I'm his uncle."

"Give him a chance. You will one day."

"So even the new tanks were inadequate?"

"Yes Pa. Seventy-five per cent of our casualties were due to mechanical failures and slow repairs. Our new Mark IIs aren't fast enough. Because railways are never reliable in war our tanks *must* be capable of moving long distances by road. The Boche succeeded because of the larger tanks, stronger armament and superior air support. Man to man I reckon we can beat him, but being dive-bombed quickly followed by tank attack is too much for an extended front."

"Do the powers that be know all this?"

"If they don't already they soon will. I'm accompanying the Brigadier to a meeting of Heads on Monday; they'll get an earful then!"

We women took no part in this talk. I do not think Adele or Babs understood much of the technicalities, though of course I did, but I said nothing.

We had so little time together as a family and Gough and I had no time at all alone. His mother and sister were not going to give him up for a moment! It brought home to me how little status I had as 'Gough's girl', and I determined to do something about it; not that I was looking for status but that it should be brought out into the open that *one day*, when Gough was ready for it, we intended to be married.

Meanwhile Gough and his father continued to talk about the war and the marvel of so many of the troops saved by the Royal Navy and fleet of little ships that had streamed across the channel from every port to pick them up.

Not all were so lucky. Denys was killed at Calais. I was sad about that.

That first meeting after Gough returned from war flew past. Just Friday and Saturday in Dolphin Square when Gough slept for twelve hours like a dead man. On the Sunday afternoon he left after driving me back to my place in his car. I had hoped for a little time together . . . but he would not come up.

"Darling," he said in the car, "I'm sorry I'm so useless, but I'll think up something before I go off again . . ."

"Where to?" I interrupted.

"*You* should know," he grimaced, the new lines in his face showing. "The re-equipping will take up all my time plus. I doubt I can get up to see the parents again; you'll have to come down to me to pick up the car. Can you make it at short notice?"

"I'll wangle it. I'm not going to miss collecting the car!" My voice was lighthearted, but my heart felt like head. Of course I knew where he would be going; one hell of a long way away, blast it.

"I'll ring. Take care; you're the one in the danger zone now."

We kissed and he drove off. To Farnborough I supposed, though I was not sure, more likely some distant training area. I felt bereft without the car. Now I would have to use the crowded public transport again. That month which Gough had spent fighting had been a luxurious one for me and fun. People turned round to look at the girl in the old Bentley! Yet that was immaterial. That he was safe in England was all that mattered.

What I did mind was that the war seemed to have come between us. The weekend had been spent doing nothing but talk war! Already Gough was totally engrossed and committed to the preparation for the next campaign to the exclusion of everything else, certainly to the exclusion of me! This, I told myself, was only to be expected. I had fallen in love with a man who was dedicated to his work. Whether it was war or peace, the army would come first. Yet he loved me. You would have thought that after all he had been through in France he'd have wanted to get on with it and marry me. Gough had once said that he needed me.

Well, if he *needed* me why didn't he . . .?

*　　*　　*

July passed excessively busily for me with long hours
working late night shifts. These sessions were more
often than not due to having to re-scramble the cipher
because the previous one had become suspect. Nine
times out of ten the Germans had not cracked the
code, but even a whiff of suspicion was enough to
have to code-scramble the whole system by re-drum-
setting the keys. It was interesting and scrupulously
exacting work. I loved it but often I returned to the
flat blurry-eyed and too tired to do more than have
the Horlicks night cap Adele had addicted me to, and
fall into bed.

Gough and I kept in touch by phone. He was
always complaining that he could never get me after
office hours and where on earth had I been so late
at night?

"Working," I would reply.

"That's an easy one."

"You have to believe me; you know it's true."

"Yes I do. You tell the truth and you are unshake-
able. But I worry. All this bombing. Do you always
go down to the shelter?"

"There, yes. We practically live in it. Here, I can't
be bothered."

"Well you bloody-well should be bothered."

"No, it's all right. Bombing not concentrated in
these parts. What about you?"

"Safe as houses in the country."

"Where in the country?"

"Silly!"

I loved these conversations with Gough. I loved to
know he worried about me as I had worried about him
when in France. They were conversations in which

neither of us could say what we were doing, yet they had an intimacy, a caring and teasing tenderness. Endearments were few, but the phone calls were to me precious love letters all of their own.

In early August a missive came from Gough: ". . . time's going on. Can't get up to London. We're frantic here preparing for the next hurdle of tank warfare. You know where – one hell of a long way to get there all the way round the Horn. I suppose there's no hope of your coming with us as undercover agent or something? I can offer you a luxurious cruise! No hope? I didn't think so. You'll have to come down here if I'm to see you again. Be prepared to drop everything at a moment's notice . . ."

I duly warned my boss. Even if he said I could not have leave I was going.

It was mid-August when the telegram came. "One way single train ticket," the message read. I knew exactly what that meant. I was to come down on Saturday morning to Taunton.

He was there in mufti on the platform to meet me. He had filled out, was brown and fit, excited to see me, and all the tension there had been on his return from France had gone. I climbed into the familiar car which felt as much mine as Gough's. The hood was open on the hot summers day. My hand rested on his thigh and the wind ruffled his hair into curls. It seemed as if the interlude of war had never happened.

"You look as beautiful as ever," he said, smiling, the wind ruffling his hair.

"You don't look too bad yourself; very handsome!"

"This time we'll beat 'em," he said.

"Where are we going?" I asked to get away from the subject of war.

"To a pub I know. Good food. By the way if I'm killed . . ."

"*Don't*. You're not going to be killed. I won't let you be," I interrupted fiercely and idiotically as if he were above the ignomy of death, but knowing only too well he was as vulnerable to the bullet and bomb as anyone made of flesh and blood. "Actually I'll allow you a small wound to get you back to blighty," I relented whimsically.

"That'd be no good. I'd be out of hospital and sent back to the front in no time. As for being disabled – I'd prefer to be killed."

"I thought we weren't going to talk war." We always seemed to come round to the wretched subject which was uppermost in our minds. I shuddered. It was impossible to contemplate that magnificent figure mutilated. "Gough, I ban the subject."

"Done," Gough said and swung the wheel to turn off the road and sweep round a drive to park before the old White Hart Inn with its views across the river to the Sinodum Hills.

We booked in, and, carrying our overnight cases found our room with its creaking floor boards and old-fashioned double bed. I looked at it curiously. It would be here . . .

We took sandwiches I had prepared in London, and, collecting a bottle of beer from the bar, made for the hills.

Leaving the car we walked some distance along a path into the countryside and sat down by a field of poppies to drink our beer and eat our meal and bask in the beauty of an English high summer with the sun hot on our backs. The fields were mostly harvested; the sweet scent of hay was in our nostrils; the blue sky above was empty and free of enemy bombers. All was very quiet.

Gough lay back with his jacket folded under his head. I thought he was asleep, but he bent over me and kissed me in the sweet way he always did, and then he parted my lips to kiss more deeply as he had once done in the flat. "A French kiss," he had called it. He had good teeth. His mouth tasted of beer and I felt a tingling awakening of lusciousness for him. He kissed me again and now there was nothing tender in the kiss which was hard and took my breath away and made me soft and supple in his arms. A slow delight crept deliciously over me.

"Say you love me. You do love me, darling, don't you . . .?" Gough murmured undoing the buttons of my blouse and kissing my neck and breasts.

"I love you Gough . . . right from the beginning." I tightened my arms around him, the stubble of the hard field prickling into my back. "I suppose you love me too?"

"You suppose right, my dearest one, and *I* also loved you right from the beginning as you know very well. You have the sweetest breasts . . ."

He was kissing my neck and I was fondling his thick head of hair, and I was dreamingly thinking how odd that this was happening to me in a field open to the sky, when the nearby barking of a dog brought us back to the fact that we were close to a public path.

"Damn and blast!" Gough cursed, moving aside.

I sat up and hurriedly buttoned my blouse and straightened my skirt. Gough looked at my flushed

153

face and lifting a comic eyebrow pulled some straw out of my hair. The dog, a black and tan spaniel, bounded over with flapping ears. I watched Gough stroking the animal with his long fingered sensitive hands.

"Shall we have a dog?" I asked.

"Rather. A friendly spaniel just like this one. No, I think I prefer labradors."

We watched as a couple with child came wandering along below us.

"Good-afternoon," we said politely.

"Lovely day," the man replied. The woman smiled and took hold of the child's hand in a protective move.

"Nice couple," Gough said. "That's us in the future."

"Oh yes," I said. "Oh Gough I do hope so."

We collected the remains of our picnic and began to retrace our steps.

"That was the most unconventional thing that has ever happened to me," I remarked as we walked down the track towards the car, "to be caught – well, *nearly* caught . . ."

". . . in the act! But special, don't you think? And erotic. We must try it out again in a field, preferably with a haystack to shelter us from viewers. First let us choose a softer nest . . ."

We could not get back to the hotel fast enough. I had never known Gough so aroused, and this set me on fire. I gloried in the fact that it was I who had abandoned myself to him on a hillside with the result I ached for him to finish what we had started with every inch of my body in a madness that threw all conventionality away in the desire and

154

the urgency. We leapt up the hotel stairs two steps at a time. Gough turned the key of the bedroom door on the inside and stood against it laughing, wild-eyed, hair all over the place while I collapsed panting onto the bed.

With my heart in my eyes I watched him come towards me. He took my hands and turning them over kissed both palms and then began to undo the blouse buttons all over again. We kissed lengthily and he said, "Oh, my love, love me now as I love you."

We undressed and I lay on the bed which was far more comfortable under me than the poppy field, and he moved over me warmly and very sure and tenderly and thus he ended my girlhood. He gave himself to me in a pleasure I had dreamed about without quite knowing what would happen. Only now the reality far outstripped the dream in the exquisiteness of the fulfilment of our love so long held back.

The perfect present obliterated all past memories and all thought of the future. We were the only people in the world, only his fine body moving over me and with me, eyes dark with passion, watching me, showing me, loving me all the way.

Chapter Fourteen

When the shadows of that unforgettable day were already lengthening, we bathed and changed and went downstairs to dinner. We lingered long over the meal and held hands surreptitiously under the starched table cloth, our eyes almost permanently upon one another. It must have been obvious to all in the dining-room that we were lovers – headily in love.

Afterwards we went outside to breathe the night air and look up into the black depth of the firmament and pick out the familiar stars of Orion and the Great Bear; and that night it felt somehow as if those far, far away worlds were part of our own magic world. Back in our room we made love again, greedy for one another, learning about each other. The thought of our imminent parting, now impossible to banish completely from our minds, filled our love-making with a poignancy that tinged rapture into an exquisite sadness that lifted us to the heights of emotion.

I did not think I had slept at all that night, holding on as I did to every precious moment of it, but I must have for I remember the surprise of finding Gough beside me when daylight began to steal round the heavy curtains. For a while I watched him sleeping, his hair over his forehead, dark eyelashes resting on deep pools like an innocent child's.

To see such a vigorous, athletic, vital man such as Gough fast asleep, turned my heart over. With the lack of men in my life I had never seen a man sleeping before. I found myself enormously moved by the sight, my feeling turned from passion to that of a mother's watchful love for her slumbering child. Tears came to my eyes at the vulnerability of a man asleep. Unable to help myself from touching him, but not wanting to wake him from the sleep he needed for this coming day, my lips brushed his forehead. But he woke and, kissing me, felt the wet on my cheeks.

"Why are you crying?" he asked deep voiced.

"Because I love you so much, and soon . . ."

"Hush . . . we still have the morning." And he took me to him again.

We rang for tea to be brought up by a maid who drew the curtains to let the sunshine in on yet another hot midsummer's day. We sat up in bed in our dressing gowns and shared the biscuit Gough dunked for us.

"Now we talk," Gough remarked.

"What about?"

"About something you need to know to understand what a foolish man I am."

"Foolish?"

"The ideal I set myself when I met you the second time was to bring my virgin bride in white very properly down the aisle once I was 'on the strength' and my CO had given his consent. All that has gone by the board with this bloody war. I believe Babs told you about how my father introduced Ben and myself to his set-up in London when we were still at school?"

"Yes. I though it a bit odd for an Englishman. Rather Continental?"

"There's French blood in Pa's veins, hence our darkness. He's a randy old man. But he loves Ma. They are so sweet together. Over the years they've come to an understanding, and when he's with her he doesn't drink as he does in London when she's not there. He would be devastated if anything happened to her. Well, Ben took the sex lessons in his stride, but then he was an open straightforward sort of boy not given to questioning . . ."

"And you are a romantic, as Babs once told me."

"The truth is I found the whole business with a tart, vulgar. I wished my father hadn't imposed it on me. In fact, as a result, I had some traumatic and unhappy years, worrying about my sexuality – but was too ashamed and mixed up to talk to anyone about it."

"But you got over it . . ."

". . . when I met my most lovely Miss Isabelle de Montfort and fell in love *au coup de foudre* as they say. With you I discovered I was a normal male and all the demons vanished. Now it seems ridiculous how I could have ever got myself in such a stew! Are you shocked at my confession?"

"It's not a confession. Nothing happened. All in the mind."

"You are so strong and sensible" he smiled. "I wanted you to know before I go how my need for you has been intense all along."

"I'm glad we waited, though I never quite understood why you were so disciplined in holding back, I mean in the flat or in the car," I replied.

"I suppose out of respect for you and the rules

you'd been brought up with. Also my romantic streak wanted to wait for marriage . . ."

"And now you've ruined that scene!" I teased.

"I'll make it up by marrying you at the very first opportunity." And he took me into his arms again.

There was a silence in the room for a while, and then we rose, dressed, and went down to face the day and the agony of separation it would bring, knowing that he was going to war and that we might never see each other again.

It was still morning when I dropped Gough outside some ugly wire gates of a depot. Inside I spied a large assembly of armoured vehicles, heavily camouflaged. We kissed in full view of the guard, who, tactfully, pretended not to notice.

Without a word we parted and I drove off alone on the road to London. I felt Gough standing there watching me go, but I did not turn round for I could not bear to see the tall figure I knew so intimately standing there on his own in the dusty road. The whole panorama of war was before him again, and this time with no illusions left of what that entailed. To my mind a second departure into war after a cracking defeat by an army superior in every way, needed tremendous nerve and courage. Those qualities Gough had in abundance.

As for me I felt the parting more poignantly than I had the first time he went to war, for now I knew the man in depth: I knew the beauty of his body, his fears, his weaknesses. The knowledge rounded him in my eyes from the previous hero figure to one which was his true self, one who genuinely needed my integrity and moral support. I would never let him down.

I became so blinded by my tears, the lump in my throat so heavy, that round a corner a little way ahead from where the ugly depot gates were hidden from view, I had to halt by the roadside. There I gave way to heart-felt sobs.

An elderly man passing on a bicycle seeing a woman in such straits, stopped. "Are you alright, Miss?" he asked leaning on his bike.

"As all right . . . as one can be . . . when one's man goes off to war," I gulped.

"I knows it all from before," he grunted, his voice sympathetic. "Boche at it again. Third time in seventy years in Europe. Time they were beaten so 'ard they can never come back with their tricks. The only way to deal with the 'un is to castrate the lot," he spat out. "With a bit 'o luck 'e'll come back to you. Take heart, Miss." He peddled off.

I had to smile. It was good to be in the country. I loved my own people. I too was doing my bit in the huge effort of the whole population, now that we had our backs to the wall, the greatest threat of all starvation through the U-boat menace in the Atlantic and all round our coast. I wiped my eyes and drove on, waving to the old man as I passed him to show I was 'alright'.

Three days later, on August 21 to be exact, Gough sailed on the *Duchess of Belfast* with his regiment from Liverpool. The tanks travelled independently on three fast merchant ships.

*   *   *

On September 7 the Blitz on London started in earnest. All hell was let loose. At first I was very frightened and every time the siren wailed scurried down to the Holland Park Underground if I was at home. Soon, mostly through tiredness and lack of sleep, I gave up going out and stayed in the comfort of my eyrie. Too bad if a bomb hit the house.

The nights were terribly noisy, but in some measure one grew accustomed to the racket and slept through, only awakened when a particularly loud blast landed somewhere dangerously near which rocked my building. The bombs were more usually aimed well away from where I lived, most of them at the docks in the East End and the estuary. I prayed that the Isle of Dogs, the scene of Gough's and my re-meeting, and where Adele now went regularly to help out, was not being especially targetted. I knew the people there would cope stoically with the discomforts and dangers. *My* people again.

Occasionally, after working late, I would go and spend the night with Adele and Geoffrey in Dolphin Square. This, as much as sticking to my promise to Gough to 'keep an eye on them', was to exchange any news we had of him, and for me to hear the latest on Babs who was expecting another baby.

About a month after Gough left I received a letter from him posted in Capetown. He sounded in great heart. Apparently they were having a riotous time on board and much deck sport to keep them fit. All were in high good humour and raring to go against the enemy of Mussolini's massed troops in Libya. Adele wanted to read the letter.

I arrived late at Dolphin Square, parked the car round the corner, and went up to the flat in the lift.

Geoffrey, in his dressing gown, opened the door to me, a glass in his hand. I got quite a shock. In the shadows of the dim black-out hall light, I thought for a moment it was Gough. As I have mentioned before, father and son were not dissimilar. He took my coat from me and I noticed he was more than unsteady on his feet.

"Adele gone to bed?" I asked when looking round the drawing-room and not seeing her.

"Called to Great Oaks. S'ad to go down to sh . . . ort problem out." He went over to the drinks cabinet and poured me out a sherry half-missing the glass, and then spilling more as he handed it to me. He splashed whisky into his near empty glass. It was obvious he had been drinking heavily, a thing he never did when Adele was in the house.

"You should have rung me and put me off," I said wiping the stem of my glass free of drips with my handkerchief.

"Did I? Perhaps I did . . . pput you off. Can't remember," he said blurrily. He waved an admonishing finger at me. "Shilly girl. Watche'it matter? I like lovely girls . . . Gough's girl. Sit down." He pushed me towards the sofa and himself sat down breathing heavily beside me.

I had never seen Geoffrey so drunk before. A bit tipsy and flirtatious yes, but always very much under control. I took a gulp of sherry and decided to leave at the first opportunity.

"I brought Gough's letter for Adele to read," I said showing it to him. He looked at it stupidly. "From Gough," I repeated loudly as if he were deaf.

"Gough?" he queried. "Gough's at sea. Specs; where's my specs?" He felt in his dressing gown pocket and did not find them.

"Here," I took the letter from him, "I'll read it to you." He seemed to take it in; at any rate some of it.

"Good fun. Good fun with the chaps. Thashs good." He drained his glass as if it were water and got up to pour himself some more.

"Don't you think you've had enough?" I said rapidly drinking my sherry. I sat on the edge of the sofa. The keys of the car were in my coat pocket in the hall.

"Time to go," I said lightly.

"No, no," he came back to the sofa and gulped the neat whisky down. He hiccoughed. "Don't leave me." He put a restraining hand over my arm. "Lonely me. Don't like being alone . . . left alone, poor me. You's a lovely girl. Really lovely. Cut above t'others. I like pretty women. Shstay wi' me. Cuddle. Nice and warm."

I hesitated. There was no harm in staying a few moments more. He was a lonely old man this father of Gough's whom I was fond of and who had always been kind and welcoming to me in his home.

"Just for a moment then." I put my empty glass down and sat back and let him put his arm over my shoulder. I thought how nice it was to have a man's arm about me again even if he *was* drunk, and how terribly I missed Gough, even more than ever since our love had been consummated. I missed him so much it was a constant ache. Yes, Geoffrey's arm over my shoulder was comforting. A very big man who oozed drink and sex appeal as he slouched beside me. His embrace tightened.

Before I had barely become aware of what was happening I found myself pinned to the sofa with Geoffrey lying on me. I resisted him and fought him.

163

But he was too heavy for me and my attempts to escape his embrace made no impact at all. In fact my struggles only made matters worse. The more I resisted, the more it seemed to encourage him as he tore at my underclothes and groped for me. He did not attempt to kiss me, thank God. It was for one thing and one thing only. I gave up struggling and tried to think it was Gough, but it was not Gough it was Geoffrey.

It was ghastly, terrible, a dreadful thing to happen with anyone other than my beloved Gough, but with his *father* – indescribably awful . . . unspeakable.

It was soon over; so quickly that later I began to almost think I had imagined it; only the shame I felt showed it was all too true. Hurriedly I collected myself and fled. Looking back from the door in fear that Geoffrey would come after me, I saw the grossness of his figure sprawled on the sofa oblivious of me or what he had done. He was already snoring.

With shaking hands I put on my coat, shut the door as quietly as I could behind me, and, running down the stairs, drove myself through the blitz of that nightmare night. I drove like a madwoman through the town lit up by searchlights and raging fires, with the raucous sounds of police alarms and ambulance sirens, to the haven of my flat. There I tore off my clothes and took a bath.

I blamed myself every bit as much for what had happened. I must never, *never* tell Gough. I had betrayed him, Gough, whom I loved beyond everything and everyone. Should he ever know it would kill his love for me, and almost as bad, kill his love for his father. None of us three would ever be able to look at one other in the eye again; the family unity which I particularly treasured, would be destroyed.

However much I tried to wriggle out of it and tell myself it was rape – and it *was* rape – I also blamed myself for not seeing what was coming.

Next morning I left for the office as usual. At lunch time Geoffrey phoned me there. What had happened, he asked? He could not remember anything after opening the door to me.

"Whatever happened," he said, "I apologize profusely. You see when Adele rang to say she wasn't coming back that night, I decided to get blind drunk. I'd forgotten you were coming. You shouldn't have seen me in that state. Gough wouldn't have liked it. Very sorry, m'dear."

"I, I . . . left," I said, "after reading you Gough's letter. That was the reason for my visit. Did you take it in?"

"No," he said. "I'd like to read it."

"Another time. I left you asleep on the sofa. Thought I'd better get home. Nothing happened."

"So sorry m'dear. Can't have made a pretty sight. Please, forget it."

I did not think he was covering up. On reflection I genuinely did not think so. On subsequent meetings I believe I would have noticed some sort of mortification, some glint of embarrassment. But there was nothing. He had been already pretty far gone when I had arrived, and he was flat out when I left. A heavy drinker at the best of times, he must have consumed an awful lot that night – a whole bottle. Then, too, had he remembered the details of that encounter I am pretty sure he would not have brought the subject up by apologizing again when we met on being 'bloody drunk'. "You see m'dear, Adele was not there and I can't stand being alone at nights – not since the Somme, and when I was wounded at Cachy in a Whippet Tank. I was with Cotton. He saved me from a grizzly death. But I . . . well, one can never forget that and the gas. Nerve goes. Adele understands . . ."

I understood then, too, about them – the family – and how the Great War had coloured their lives and left lasting damage. Yes, I understood why Geoffrey got drunk when he was alone, and why he had to have women, but the knowledge did not assuage my guilt which I had to learn to live with.

Chapter Fifteen

I heard through the office that Gough's regiment with all equipment had arrived safely and disembarked at Port Said. I imagined Gough having a quick look round the port with its colourful *souks* and its famous Simon Arts Store from where his men would buy cheap gifts to send home for Christmas.

Had Gough from the ship watched the brown-skinned boys diving naked for pennies? Had he listened to the gully-gully men gabbling away in their rapid pidgin English? Did he briefly take a ride on a camel, visit a mosque, watch the crowds dressed in long white *galabeahs*, red fezzes on thick thatches of black hair?

Later I heard that Gough had briefly done all these things before entraining for the Western Desert for a couple of months of extensive exercise in a remote part. This open fighting ground was as different as one could get from what he had experienced in Europe, and he was also up against a different enemy, the Italians, who had entered the war on the side of Germany in that same June that the BEF had been forced out of France.

Gough's unit was destined to join the 7th Armoured Division, the 'Desert Rats' already famous, as was their Commander-in-Chief General Sir Arthur Wavell. By the time Gough arrived, many battles had been won and morale was high despite the fact that the British forces were puny in the extent of the vast expanses of desert to be defended.

At last came Gough's first letter from the desert:

22/10/40
Darling,

Will you thank the parents for me for their cables? I haven't received a letter yet from any of you, and doubt if you have received one of mine as none of us out here have yet had any acknowledgements. They not only starve us of decent rations in wartime, they starve us of letters from home! The postal system out here seems to have broken down, partly, I suppose, because they can't spare any aeroplanes.

This is an extraordinary place, out of this world, quite beautiful at times with the most magnificent sunsets and sunrises you could possibly imagine. I am very fit. The worst part are the flies. As we are miles and miles from anywhere one wonders where they come from. They cluster disgustingly on cups and fall into our mugs. The biggest local unpleasantness is due to them, I guess. Most of the chaps succumb to suffering from tummy, and I expect it will be my turn next, but I am told one soon gets over it and becomes acclimatized. Hard rations are fearfully dull and unpalatable, i.e. biscuits, bully beef – made into a stew – tinned rations and tea. Water is rationed at half a gallon per head per day, and is more important than food. As a result we don't wash much!

In the middle of the day it is piping hot (100°F or so) and very cold at night. Shirt sleeves and shorts are the order, with everything you can put on at night. We go to bed *very* early as we can't show lights here – wrapped up like mummies in blankets. Average bed time is 8 p.m., sometimes 7! Blast these flies; so impertinent, they sit on eyelids and lips until brushed off. I have dozens crawling over me in my office as I write. Some office! It is a lean-to of canvas set up against my tank, a Roorkee chair and low table for furniture.

For a change from desert training I managed to get one blissful bathe in when visiting a seaside town. (Can't say anything as to where as you know). The novelty was improved upon by the fact that the town was bombed by the Ities while we were in the water! I gather the Hun is bombing you. Please take the greatest care, my love. At this slow rate of mail I had better send A Very Merry Christmas message to you all now! I long for a letter.

Always your Gough.

After a gap another letter from Gough arrived, dated November 5; a date that had, at the time, no especial significance to Gough but one which had, by the time his letter arrived, become the blackest day of my life up until then. I will just copy out what I wrote on that date in my diary:

November 5

A ghastly thing has happencd. It is now dark. I am back in the flat yet I still cannot take in that what I saw isn't a nightmare from which I shall awake. At the same time my brain tells me it is horribly true.

At 5 o'clock this morning a bomb hit Dolphin Square. One of the neighbours in another house rang me up. I threw on some clothes and rushed over in Gough's car. "A direct hit on the corner of one of the blocks high up" is what the man said over the phone. He did not say *which* House. He had no need to; otherwise why should he have rung *me*? The fire engines were there by the time I arrived. I could only stand and watch with the crowd the extended ladders reaching to the top of the building. From where I stood I could see some of the familiar furniture exposed in the huge gap. They got Geoffrey out first, then Adele. They put them on the ground and went on to save the living. I knelt down beside them and forced myself to pull back the coverings so that I could tell Gough. Adele's face looked serene and untouched, caught for eternity in her sleep as indeed she had been. The rest of her small body was pathetically mutilated. Geoffrey was unrecognizable, grey-hair blood-matted. He had taken the full blast. Was this what Gough's body would look like if . . .? An appalling premonition spread with sickening nausea over me. At the same time I felt relief that my terrible secret was safe for all time. I found myself shivering violently.

They took the bodies away and gave me the name of the hospital. They asked me who I was and I said an old family friend and that I would inform the next of kin, but still I knelt on where they had been. I loved them as if they were my own parents. I loved Geoffrey as Gough's father. Death obliterates what happened between us. I knelt on stunned and shaking until a woman from another House, Nelson I think it was, took me into her apartment and gave me a cup of tea. After a while I drove myself back to my place and rang Babs in Scotland. It was still early and fortunately I got Angus. He said he would come down straight away and would stay in Bailey's Hotel – the hotel his family used when in London – and to meet him there later that day. He would not allow Babs to come in her pregnant condition. There was nothing more I could do. I went to work as usual. It is a complete nightmare.

Meanwhile Angus arrived. He was an absolute brick. We met next day at the hotel and he arranged everything from cabling Gough to identifying the bodies in the mortuary and seeing the family solicitor in the City. Neither of the parents' wills said anything about a burial so with Babs' consent we arranged to have a private cremation. We asked the undertakers to hold the ashes until such time that they could be taken to the chapel in the grounds of Great Oaks Hall and laid in Ben's grave.

I wrote to Gough. I knew he would be absolutely devastated. I offered to try and come out to him if that would help though I knew my chances of getting to his Front were slim. My brain appeared to have seized up temporarily and I found it difficult to grasp what date it was; so much had happened in that year, which seemed the longest in my life.

But it was still 1940 when I received that second letter from Gough. On its arrival I got another shock in the address on the letter which read: 'Officers Section. 2/5th General Hospital, Egypt'. I tore it open and devoured the first page, reading with blessed relief:

. . . hope my address doesn't give you too much of a shock. Actually I am quite recovered and should be up tomorrow. Fancy being in hospital out here without yet being in battle. Shocking! I succumbed to the prevailing tummy trouble which the MO suspected was appendicitis. I might just as well have been a wounded soldier being bundled off in agony on a nightmare journey from miles and miles out in the blue. I was carted about into five different motor ambulances and an ambulance train! The first thirty to forty miles of my motor ride was across country. No roads or even tracks and the desert is quite rocky, not a bit what it sounds. It was absolute hell. Anyway after a starvation diet of water only (well and truly boiled) the thing subsided and they decided not to operate, so I am now being fed like the fatted calf and am perfectly fit again and very keen to get back to my men after a few days of recuperation in civilization. I hope to get some river sailing there at the local club and go in for some races. You can guess where!

All I will have missed with the unit is a few desert storms so I'm not worrying about that and am enjoying the rest and being *clean* again! I reckon I had my first long bath with fresh water since *our* hotel in Taunton. Ah, blissful times, *n'est pas* my darling?

They are extraordinarily good in this hospital. Most of the doctors are Harley Street physicians and surgeons when not at war. Quite a few of the sisters and the two doctors who examined me are naval people, and very efficient and nice they are too. It augurs well for the casualties bound to come. We'll show the Italians, and if Rommel's victorious troops turn up here, as rumour has it, we'll show them too! The present dampener is the number of Italian aircraft swooping over us in the desert. Like the flies they seem to have no trouble in finding where we are. So far little opposition in the air from us. The cry is where is the bloody RAF? Rumour has it there are only three Lysanders available. At least they three could bring us the mail! All Gladiators are withdrawn.

I'll send this letter by air mail but is it really any quicker? Many don't think so. One feels so terribly cut off. I've had no direct news from England since coming out except for the two cables mentioned in my last from the parents saying all well and that includes *you*, thank God. Some people here have only just got letters dated from June and July – *five* months! Truly the wheels of the Postal Service grind slowly. It really is a disgrace as the troops worry and it is bad for morale.

All love . . .

The letter was penned from hospital on the same day

his parents were killed and Angus sent a cable to him. The cable chased Gough out into the desert; was forwarded to the hospital; missed him there and again in Alexandria during his short recuperative leave, after which, and still unaware of the double tragedy, Gough went into action. Perhaps it was just as well that the cable never reached him. He was in euphoric mood when he rejoined his unit and prepared for the romp of his career from which he was to come out covered in glory.

Gough's campaign began late in that year of 1940 when an army of tanks gathered deep in the desert. He dressed in the individual gear which the tank commanders tended to sport, and I was subsequently told how Gough, in the lead with his squadron, looked every inch a desert hero. He wore brown suede desert boots with rubber soles, beige corduroy trousers, khaki shirt with brown leather coat to waist over. Round his neck was tied with flair a silk muffler in Wykehamist colours. Goggles and the famous black beret completed the outfit. Those who commanded him on the campaign said he looked magnificent up there in his turret as he led. Adored by his men, and admired by his fellow officers they said he radiated optimism and utter fearlessness.

On that December day, at dusk, they set forth. There were tanks spearing ahead, tanks on either side, and tanks behind shrouded in clouds of sandy dust. Pennants fluttered and strained from the wireless aerials. In each turret a man's dark head could be seen silouetted black against the lowering horizon. Late, this army of ships on a dry land, floated over a vanishing mirage. Later still they leaguered for refuelling and a brew-up before the crews snatched a few hours sleep beside their vehicles during which time the officers were briefed as to the latest situation.

Then off before dawn in a howling red *simoon* sandstorm that had arisen in the night, headphones on, voices crackling over the turbulent air. Gough, with now three months desert experience behind him, knew the difference between the hot *khamseen* sand storms of Egypt and this icy wind of winter with its columns of whirling dust, its putrid smell, and the clatter and clamour it brought as it whirled stones against vehicles, strained guy ropes to their limits and tore at canvas lean-tos until they took off. Sand got into eyes, noses, mouths, ears, food and water; it got into every aperture even though men were muffled up to look like Moslem women wearing yashmaks, or something out of the Arab Legion.

Daylight revealed the spectacular sight as far as the eye could see of the whole desert covered with a mass of dispersed vehicles of the Eighth Army all rolling along in a turbulent sea of dust and hazy visibility. The army on the move made a sure target for enemy aircraft. The British this time were lucky. Due to the sand storm there were none overhead.

The advance carried on, eight miles to the hour, the storm dying away. The last approach to the line-up area was carried out by moonlight. With the weather now clear, the tank commanders navigated by the stars. Even in this Gough seemed to be pre-destined to be where he was. As a boy he had sailed with his parents, Babs and Ben to the Mediterranean where they hugged the North African coast as far as Alexandria before turning back to Malta. Gough's childhood introduction to the stars in that latitude served him well for desert navigation.

Now, as the distance from the Italian Army lessened and narrowed, there came a deep silence over the air. The timing in the meeting of the enemy was vital. In the dark the tanks halted and waited for the Infantry to come up and precede them. Gough in the leading wave of tanks held back so as to arrive at the objective twenty minutes ahead of the Infantry whom they would overtake on the way. The second wave of tanks coming up behind him aimed to arrive only just ahead of the Infantry.

Having navigated a round-about course, Gough's regiment went straight into the attack at the most northerly point on the coast at Sidi Barrani between Mersa Matruh and Tobruk where the Italians were dug into a chain of strongly fortified camps high up on the dunes, the sea on their port side sparkling below them.

On that December day the first desert battle in which Gough partook did not last long. Italian resistance soon collapsed before such determination and skill. It was the very opposite of the experience encountered in France. Here the village of Sidi Barrani with its dug in fortifications was left shattered, more than a hundred defensive guns overrun. In all 2,500 prisoners were taken to cause more trouble to the tank men than had the fighting. No one had foreseen prisoners-of-war in such numbers. The regiment waited around guarding them until trucks came to take the captured away and leave the tank men free to forge on down the coast westwards.

Gough's first letter after being in action arrived:

. . . dog-tired, but functioning well. Been at it non-stop for eight days and haven't removed my clothes for twelve! You can imagine what sort of fun we have been having! I expect you will have read of some of the events in the papers. The Regiment has been in the thick of it from the beginning and once more I say, my God my men are marvellous. In the face of this sort of conflict we all know what might at any moment happen to us – and it is not a pretty sight. One's friends within seconds become not how we knew them so well but unrecognizable remains of torn and bleeding tissue. I hope I am not distressing you. It is a relief to tell someone. The stiff upper lip is the only face I show here. Don't mention any of this to the parents. Lying under the stars at night I wonder how God can let this happen to mankind again and again . . . forgive me darling for pouring it out to you.

Later. Same letter. No chance to post it. Still December I suppose. Christmas got lost this year. I hope you all had a happy time together. I haven't heard for so long. I'm a captain now, three pips up. *On the strength*! What about coming out to marry me! Fat lot of use that would be with me stuck in the desert.

People expect it to be hot in the desert in winter. More like the South Pole! Nights are cold, cold, cold, the hard ground under one, penetratingly so, despite ground sheet. I know what it must feel like to be in a grave.

Well now that the Ities are on the run our routine is that after days at it when they halt from the chase to fight, we pull out and take ourselves off into our own little bit of desert, far away from trouble, where we make a village of tanks. Pretty it is, our village; home to us, and fun. We sleep, eat, talk over the latest battle, joke, shave off the week-old beards. Would you like me with a beard? A fuzzy one with some red in it. Now, where did I get that from? Some throwback I imagine!

Still later. The Regiment has done pretty well they all tell us, and though our 'horses' are a bit weary we are all in good form. The big bangs go off quite close to where we are now which is rather disturbing, but they have not succeeded in puncturing us yet! War changes one. I have become hardened to it. Though not when those are killed on our side whom we know; for instance one of our commanders the other day, a great man. One never gets callous about that. I am to take over from him.

On the other hand the enemy's bodies mean little. But their wounded, quite different reaction; we give the enemy exactly the same treatment as we give our own. We do the first aid, give them our rations and look after them as best we can until the ambulances come along. They are not only poorly dressed but seem to be half-starved. They are pathetically grateful. I am much in demand as I speak Italian. Did you know it was one of my subjects at school? Pa and Ma were keen on us learning languages. French too and a spattering of German.

Jack Daly, one of the boys whom you met at Lulworth, was killed at Sidi Barrani. He was a good friend of mine. I had to write to his people. Pat Hobson takes over; another one you knew. We had to bury the crew from C Squadron; the gunner and operator were dead inside, the driver and his commander in bits; tank burnt out. Tanks don't blow up, they burn. They also smell of cordite. The crew sometimes pass out, from the fumes of cordite, after firing their guns due to the lack of ventilation down there. I shouldn't be telling you all this but you are strong . . . don't tell the parents though – nor anything bloody. Dad had enough of that in the last war.

Later again. Now, AT LAST a letter from you and a *parcel*. Marvellous, even though written soon after I left UK. Thanks awfully for the chocs, socks, and 3 paperback 'whodunits' to take my mind off the present. My word it was welcome. Briefing in CO's HQ any moment. Off again at 05.00 hrs. Here goes!

Your G.

Though I would not have wanted Gough to write less openly to me, I found parts of his letters distressing. I too had seen mutilated bodies as the result of bombing and not only Geoffrey's and Adele's but others being extracted from bombed buildings. The East End, and in particular the dockland area which I still visited from time to time, was in a terrible mess. Yes, I too knew the destruction and maiming of war whether in the open desert or in a city like London. I waited, as time went on, fearful for Gough's reaction to the news of his parents' deaths.

Chapter Sixteen

The letters from the Middle East continued to come long after events had taken place. Saddest of all for Babs were Gough's letters to their parents which I arranged to be forwarded straight on to her. We discussed over the phone sending a second cable but thought better of the idea.

Life for me in London plodded on. Without Adele and Geoffrey with whom to exchange news, I threw myself more than ever into my work. We had had a great stride forward with the introduction of a secure British cipher which meant we were closed to the Germans. Though there was always a slight doubt, I had nothing like so much rescrambling to do. My main job now was to unscramble *them*!

Meanwhile, Gough continued to prove his mettle out in the Field. After Sidi Barrani he was promoted to Major, and was thus in a position to play a pivotal role in the strategic Battle of Beda Fomm which took place on February 5, 1941, in which twenty thousand Italian prisoners were taken.

It was during this crucial time of danger that four of Gough's tanks were badly hit including his own which was incapacitated. He was left trapped, a sitting target raked by fire. Then David Willis, his second-in-command whom I had known at Bovington, quick to see from his tank what was happening to his CO, arrived in the midst of the pounding barrage and managed to extracate Gough from the broken turret. Amazingly Gough was unhurt. He immediately leapt into David's tank and took up command again.

For his part, Gough was put in for an immediate DSO and David Willis, who had rescued him under heavy fire, an immediate MC. In all, the British had only three thousand troops against the thousands and thousands of Italians who had fought bravely and well throughout the day. It was said that at Beda Fomm Gough had displayed a classic sense of battle. He had not had time to study the ground before but instinctively took in the lay-out and acted on it brilliantly.

The Battle of Beda Fomm was declared the first great triumph of the Royal Armoured Corps in the desert. Churchill sent congratulatory messages and a new version of his famous phrase of 'The Few' was coined. The British Press, desperate for good news, was euphoric: 'This first campaign in North Africa', I read in London in *The Times*, 'is a magnificent achievement with a string of victories in the face of vastly superior numbers. General Graziani's Army was wiped out. The Battle of Beda Fomm is a classic example of armoured warfare, brilliantly led by our young experienced commanders'.

Gough's first letter after the battle was typical in its understatement about his part in it, but full of euphoria:

. . . we have, since I last wrote, finished no ordinary battle of which you will no doubt have read about in the newspapers. About a fortnight ago I gave up Adjutant and took over command of the squadron. Little did I know how lucky I was to get promotion to Major at exactly that time! I can only say here that we were in action from 9.30 a.m. until 6 p.m. without any rest at all. We undoubtedly won the most decisive victory against much superior numbers. The Bn. has had the most delightful things said about it by everyone, and my squadron in particular. We are all pretty chuffed just now! We will have to rest and refit soon, as our horses are few and pretty battered, but until that time comes we are well stocked up with Italian food and drink and will any moment be dashing off down the road again with no expected resistance.

The men of my squadron have been simply magnificent; so have the officers. David W., whom you knew and who is my 2nd i/c, rescued me from a very nasty situation when I got stuck, tank knocked out, with all hell let loose round. You will know doubt say God Bless David as I do! He deserves, and I am sure will get, a medal. But don't worry. None of this will go to our heads. Too much unpleasantness for that. One of my chaps, a South African lad by the name of Bill Frank may have to have an arm amputated, and one of my L/Cpls has lost the sight of an eye. The rest of us in the squadron miraculously got away with it.

I *can* tell you about the weather. For the last few days b – y awful. Real stormy and wet including hail! It is raining like sin at the moment and is perishing cold under a canvas sheet beside a small truck which is our officers' Mess. Talk about tropical rain; you can't see more than 50 yds through it and it is blowing horizontally! Too wet to continue this letter . . .

It was shortly afterwards, following a briefing of Gough's squadron, that his Brigadier asked him to stay behind. The Brigadier, whom they called 'Blood' made him sit down, gave him a drink and broke the news of his parents' death in the London bombing. Gough wrote the letter I had been dreading whilst on the long trek back to base:

. . . the Brigadier must often deal with this sort of thing. He is as tough as blazes in war and yet could not have been more gentle and kind in telling me about it and about the cable which had been resurrected from somewhere to land on his table. He asked if I wanted compassionate leave though he said he doubted I would get it as it is only given to the UK in very exceptional circumstances, and seasoned commanders like myself are too thin on the ground to let go. I said No. What is the good? It is so *long* ago. What hurts most at the moment is that all this time that I have been writing them letters, I did not *know*, had no inkling. One would have thought that with parents as close as we were I would have had some sort of intuition all was not well, but nothing.

I can't bear the thought of you having had to deal with it on the spot. I am sure you must have rushed over. Oh, darling I should have been there. The last letter I have had from you must have been written just before – same with one from Babs dated January. Don't let anyone but Babs see my letters to them will you? Death is so near here that one comes to expect it, but not at home, not where *you* are.

A week later I am still stunned by the news. I don't seem to be able to take it in all this way away, yet I know it to be true. I long to cry like a baby, but where can one weep in a mess lean-to with other men? My sleep is troubled by hideous dreams of the parents' end and then I wake in the icy dawn to be pierced again by the terrible knowledge of what has happened . . . that they are no longer there to turn to . . . they were good parents – the best. They would have been so pleased with my medal. It was for them, and for my men.

Can you come? Will you try and come? You and Babs are all I have left now. Babs should be safe in Scotland with her children and with Angus to comfort her, but you . . . Oh God, I feel sick every time I think of you in London in the bombing. Please, please, my precious one, take every care. Come out if you can. I need you so badly, and you'll be safer here. Write c/o GHQ Middle East. In time it will find me. I want all the details. I know you will have written . . .

My letters did eventually catch up with him, and he thanked me for them, but he never referred to his parents' deaths again. I knew how deep the double tragedy had hit.

Chapter Seventeen

I went to Mr Williams, still my civilian boss. "Not a hope," he said with apparent total disregard for my feelings and wishes.

"Why not a hope?"

"Because there are no family postings to the Middle East, that's why. Cairo is a no-go area. If you were a wife you might have got a passage to Cape Town. Husbands can sometimes get leave to go there from GHQ, ME, but you're not a wife. What would you do hanging around for the Major to come for ten days' leave and then probably get no more? Anyway I'm not letting you go, not now we've got the hang of these new codes."

"You can't keep me on for ever," I said stubbornly.

"For the duration I can. Never forget you're under the Official Secrets Act for life. You knew the rules perfectly well when you joined."

I did, and about one of our girls who was parachuted into France, captured by the Gestapo and tortured for what they could get out of her. Afterwards she was shot. I shivered.

"Could I get a similar job to mine in Cairo?" I tried another tack. Surely all I'd learnt at the War Office would be useful in other headquarters?

"You're not in uniform."

"I could enlist."

"If you did you'd be sent to Bletchley Park or one of the other Intelligence establishments in this country. 'Mr Williams' cold blue eyes stared.

"If anything suitable job-wise comes through for the Middle East, I'd be obliged— "

"Yes, yes," he abruptly cut me off. "Now, get on with this." And he handed me a file marked 'Top Secret'.

I had no intention of letting the matter go. Gough wanted me; needed me. Even if he left Egypt for a new front further East where there had been a disaster in Crete I would be nearer to him out there. I would step up my letters to Gough – and somehow bide my time.

Six months passed. Gough was much in action with the 7th Armoured Brigade in an ebb and flow type of warfare against their old enemy Rommel who had come with his Afrika Korps to the rescue of the Italians. The German general was, Gough rediscovered, a far tougher proposition than the latter. To add to the difficulties in Gough's case, though his RTR had been re-equipped with reconditioned Crusader tanks these were often found to be in a shaky and unreliable condition.

There ensued a string of clashes all the way from Benghazi eastwards to the stubborn battles in and around Tobruk. Sometimes the British gained ground, usually they lost it. In his letters there were veiled references of 'incompetence in high places', and sometimes more directly of a 'bloody balls-up at the top'.

I gathered he was constantly being ordered to deploy his tanks in a manner which in his view could only be disadvantageous to the British. Again and again he and the other squadron commanders were forced back when they reckoned had they been allowed to use their own methods according to the ground they found themselves on, they need not have retreated. Gough, with his experience of Rommel in France reckoned he knew enough of the wiley old Fox's mind to see what he was up to in various situations and how he could be deflected.

One thing that erked Gough more than anything at this time was the lack of permission to go in for night attacks, a strategy which he had used against the Italians to much advantage. What made it worse was that his unit was constantly being attacked in their leaguers at night by Rommel's forces. This meant that instead of sleeping by their tanks they were properly kept awake all night shrouded inside their uncomfortable vehicles, and they came out to do battle at daylight already tired.

At last, after months of frustration, Gough's pleading was heard by the General who had had his eye on him since Beda Fomm, and he was permitted to lead a night attack near Sidi Rezegh from which the British had been excluded. Gough arranged to lead the advance himself on foot in a complete sound and light blackout. To avoid confusion and to ensure total surprise he allowed no artillery support, but ordered bangs further away to distract and to muffle the sound of tanks on the move. A second squadron was to follow him some minutes later with an infantry battalion. He chose a pitch black night.

His force appeared in the dark from nowhere and took the enemy completely by surprise. Little resistance was encountered and the attack succeeded brilliantly with not a single tank casualty. A vital corridor was opened for the allies to the sea.

For this valuable achievement Gough was awarded a bar to his Beda Fomm DSO. He became renowned as a 'night man' who could show superb flexibility in confounding the enemy. His brilliance in the Field came under the eyes of the C-in-C himself, and he became a picked man for the Staff.

Things moved fast for Gough. He was taken away from 'the old firm', as he called his regiment, was demoted to captain and sent to the Armoured Fighting Vehicles Branch at Headquarters as GIII while waiting to go to the Middle East Staff College in Haifa on the next course in September. This meant that when there he would revert even lower to his substantive rank of subaltern.

'Why,' Gough wrote to me on the new airgraphs of little space, 'we should be selected for the Course against stiff competition on the one hand and penalized in rank with the other is just one of life's little mysteries!'

After only a week at his 'desk job', Gough was already writing that although he felt delightfully rested at AFTV HQ, it got on his nerves sitting on a stool all day working from six a.m. to eight p.m., though he did get a couple of afternoons off a week when he joined the small boat club and went sailing on the Nile where there was usually a breeze in summer temperatures that could reach 116°F.

'I miss the responsibility I've had as Squadron-Commander,' Gough wrote, 'surely the best job in the world. When recently I met my old General in the office he told me my regiment was doing splendidly and could always be relied upon to get them out of a tight spot, I nearly went mad with frustration not to be with them!'

As for myself I was filled with happiness to read these letters. I could not care less how bored or frustrated he was! My relief in the knowledge that he was out of the battle line was enormous. I wrote that it was a great honour to be selected for the Staff College, so *stop grumbling*. He wrote back to say his only real grumble was that I wasn't with him *now*. It was a terrible waste that I wasn't there. When was I coming out? '. . . it is hot and stormy and I have to wring my shirts of sweat throughout the day. There is no sailing at the moment as the Nile is in flood. You must join the club when you come. I keep fit by swimming, and I've met a man who was on the last Staff College course who said it was great fun. There was some very good duck shooting there, and the kind fellow is going to lend me his shotgun. Soon moving camp, thank God,' came his last letter from AFVHO.

I stepped up my campaign to get out to him and wondered how such a man would ever settle to 'desk work' after passing out from the Staff College.

The letters from Haifa were written in the red ink usually used by the Staff for ruthless and pertinent corrections of their students' attempts. Apparently the students had run out of blue ink!

> . . . this is a perfectly lovely place. We are right on the top of a mountain (read your Bible and you will find out where) overlooking the sea. Pinewoods and orange orchards could not be greener and more attractive-looking in contrast to living in the Egyptian desert.

Here we stay in very comfortable little modern houses and work and feed in an hotel which has been taken over for the purpose. I'd be in danger of getting 'soft' if it were not for the steady twelve to fourteen hour day they work us. There is wonderful bathing and surf riding in warm sea, though one has to be careful not to go too far out where there are strong undercurrents. The shooting is great too. I went out at the weekend with eight other guns walking some twenty miles or so over the most frightful going. We bagged some brace of 'chikaws' – hill partridges – plus duck and snipe. The duck shooting on Lake Hule north of Galilee is out of this world.

Apart from a three day half-term break in Syria for more shooting, we shall be working right through Christmas Day. Soon after that I'm due to be released from here on ten days' leave before my next posting (don't know where yet), the first leave I'll have had since coming out fourteen months ago. MIND YOU ARE IN CAIRO THEN. At Christmas I'm going to beat it up a bit with the chaps while I am still a subaltern. After that the utmost sobriety required of a married man! My dear old 2nd, after sterling work in Tobruk, are off to stop the rot in Burma. How I wish I were with them . . .

I was desperate to get out to marry Gough for his January leave in the New Year. Then I had a break through. They were short of cipher experts in the Middle East. Mr Williams agreed to let me go. I joined the ranks of the Women's Auxiliary Territorial

Service in a lowly job, donned khaki uniform, and waited and waited and waited.

Typically of those war years I did not arrive in Egypt in time for Gough's leave. I got to a Cairo blazing with lights and nightclubs at the beginning of April 1942 by which time Gough had left. There was a letter for me with an address to which to write: HQ 7 Armoured Division, MEF. Desert again, but a staff job with rank of major, a GII to his old general. I comforted myself that at least he would be well behind the firing line.

Though he was not on the spot, literally everyone knew, or knew of, Gough Nicholson, and once again I was 'Gough's girl' come out to marry him. I was fêted and entertained in great fashion with invitations galore to dances and to dine at Shepherd's Hotel. I swam and joined the sailing club, sailing with Gough's friends.

I was more cross than anything for his not being there. I had given up my highly thought of job at the War Office, had put on an ill-fitting uniform to do some lowly typing, and Gough was nowhere to be seen! However there were letters from him which came through quickly. And, there was John: John Shawe, the boyfriend I had been with when I first met Gough at the Sandhurst Ball.

Since the outbreak of war when he was still in India, I had lost touch with him. He had come to the Middle East with his Indian troops; he had fought with them, won the MC and gone to the Haifa Staff College course preceding Gough's. He was now a major doing a staff job with the Indian contingent. In a less spectacular way his career had followed

191

Gough's, and he too loved his troops, speaking Urdu with them like a native. But there was nothing spectacular about John. Though obviously competent in war, he was quite content to stay behind the front. As a gunner he was more a technical man than a fighting man.

He looked military, though, with his small moustache. I liked him very much as I had once told him in London when he asked if I would wait for him.

He knew about Gough and that I had come out to marry him. Our friendship picked up where it had left off in London and he became my escort for all the 'do's' I was invited to in the frenzy of Cairo now threatened by the approaching German guns, which at nights could be heard blasting away.

John proved to be the best of companions. "Why aren't you married?" I asked him one day when we were dining *à deux* at Shepherd's. "You know you should be. You'd make some girl very happy." And so he would; he was quiet, had good manners, was intelligent, undemanding and totally reliable.

"I'm waiting for you to get married first, then I will," he answered with his short laugh.

"You are a dear," I said, resting my hand on his across the table, "but really you shouldn't. I'll look around for someone for you. Plenty of nice girls in my set up dying to get married!" I felt flattered and humbled by what he had said. All these years, and these two men had never deviated from their love of me. I saw myself again at seventeen in my pink salmon dress which was still in its box in my flat, and I saw myself now aged twenty-four, and I despaired. How much longer would I have to wait around for Gough to get leave?

192

Chapter Eighteen

Late in that May of 1942, a month or so after my arrival in Cairo, news was flashed through that Rommel had made a great thrust forwards with his Panzer Divisions in Gazala, and that the advanced British Headquarters in the Field had been overrun. The Staff were missing presumed taken prisoner-of-war.

This was the one event I had not considered. I had envisaged Gough being wounded or even killed – though the latter was too dreadful to dwell on more than fleetingly – but taken prisoner?

Their chance to escape came later that same day, just before dark when the German fighting unit they were with was attacked again. In the confusion Gough, his General, and the other two staff officers managed to nip out of the lorry they were held in, and scoot for an old gun emplacement about four hundred yards away. Once there they burrowed under a tarpaulin where they lay in much discomfort for three hours hardly daring to breathe, but with growing hope as the hue and cry died out when it became dark, and their captors gave up.

When they felt it was safe they crept out, found some water, and set off to walk through several enemy parties milling around. They picked their way through a good many minefields to where they thought British troops might be found. Gough with his night eyes and expert navigation lead the way. After some sixteen miles of tricky going they heard a Scottish voice challenging them and knew they were safe.

Their 'daring escape' was much talked of in Cairo, and I was congratulated on being engaged to one of the 'heroes'. Gough wrote shortly: '. . . the fortunes of war are more down than up. I had a nine hour stint in the bag with Jerry. We all got away, trust us! I've had enough excitement in the last three weeks to last me a lifetime. It will continue however. Can't say anything more now. All my love, Gough.'

If I had thought that 'being put in the bag for nine hours' would be an excuse for some leave for Gough to come and marry me, I was very much mistaken! Even if he had been offered it he would not have taken it. It was after that episode that I gave up all ideas of a wedding. For that I would have to wait until the war was over. This feeling was overwhelmingly born out by Gough's next move: he volunteered for a transfer back to the front line. His beloved 2 RTR were by now far away in the East, but the almost equally dear 6 RTR were nobly fighting along the coastal road just beyond his Advanced HQ.

Gough's General was extremely reluctant to let him go. Gough had done sterling work at Advance GHQ during the most difficult campaign of all. But fighting tank officers of Gough's calibre and experience were desperately needed to lead at the front. The men up there were not so much demoralized by the withdrawals as bemused and bewildered as to what was happening when time and again they gave of their best and in individual battles beat the enemy to it. Yet it was not enough. There had been too many casualties too many times. The General knew they were fifty per cent short of officers and men after the recent fighting. What they needed was just such a commander as Gough Nicholson to re-inspire.

So the General let Gough go. He let him go to command a squadron of 6 RTR with, in about a month's time, promotion to lieutenant-colonel and the command of the whole regiment. On the day Gough reported to his new command he went straight into action.

When I heard of Gough's posting I could feel the blood pumping fearfully through my heart. To volunteer to go back into the thick of what everyone knew was going to be the toughest battle of all to stop and contain Rommel at El Alamein, seemed to me to be almost a death wish. Would he have volunteered had we been married; had he had the son he would have been so proud of? All I knew was that if we had been married and he had succumbed to my pleading to stay on the Staff, he would have hated himself for doing so. After all I had known it would be thus. I had taken Gough on with my eyes open knowing that tanks came first.

Some said that at this time of retreat to El Alamein on the Egyptian frontier, only sixty miles from Alexandria and the Nile Delta, many had lost faith. But when Gough joined his new command he found morale gritty with determination that they could finally hold Rommel and his reduced Panzer divisions at El Alamein. He went straight into action and stayed in it for a 'slogging three week match', as he wrote, before being pulled out. There was a short rest and the fight went on; but if the British were exhausted, Rommel was ill and he was in difficulties, stopped and defeated in every direction so that there was nowhere for him to go other than to retrace his steps. He made one more punch for victory along the Ruweisat Ridge but was checked by 6 RTR and 8 RTR blocking his way during which battle the commander of the 8th had his arm shattered by a shell. Gough took over and carried on with the combined effort until Rommel abandoned the attack and the 6th and 8th were pulled out.

There was a letter from Gough, dated 9 July 1942. In it he said:

> . . . am enjoying my first day out of the fun and games. The squadron is like a dead man except for the guards, and me scribbling away to you. The day before yesterday and yesterday were great days. We knocked spots off the German tanks and infantry with many a 'maiden over'. Everyone's tail is right up I can tell you after rumours that Rommel has been forced to admit defeat and abandon the attack. I really believe that at last the tide has turned in our favour, which puts us all in great spirits. We have averaged under three hours' sleep in twenty-four over several weeks but are rapidly recovering . . .

This extract from Gough's letter was subsequently published in the British press with: 'No more convincing as well as moving piece of evidence can be had than this from a brillant and gallant young officer, on the turn of the tide in July to make victory possible next'.

He himself personally handed me this, his last, letter, a couple of days after writing it; his face, burnt dark by desert sun, creased into his familiar grin as he did so. I had not seen him since Taunton – August 1940. Now it was July 1942, nearly two years later.

He had sent a message to me in Cairo earlier. One of his teeth was giving him 'merry hell'. He was cadging a lift from his brigadier to get it attended to in civilization. I was to wait for him at the sailing club.

It was a meeting of incredible joy, of rapturous happiness, of love . . . We dined at the club and then sat out overlooking the Nile and enjoying the slight breeze as darkness fell with Gough puffing away at his pipe to keep the mosquitoes at bay. They got the better of us and drove us in and to my place where the other girls turned a discreet blind eye and, against all rules, Gough spent the night in my bed under the mosquito net and rotating punkha.

What did we do? We made love, slept, talked until Gough fell asleep again in my arms . . . made love again. It was like that time in the White Hart Inn in Taunton only even more marvellous for this time we were so near to one another across the desert. He was not going off on a long sea journey thousands of miles away. The meeting utterly confirmed to me how right it was to have come all the way around the Cape; to have dropped my good job, my pay, my everything to come out to be nearer to him was totally vindicated.

We were so full of resilience and happiness.

"Next break I'll make sure that I leave enough time to get married," he said. He repeated again his belief that the tide really had turned in the allies' favour, that Rommel had suffered losses far worse than ours, that the Germans had run out of punch, that the British really had got them trapped between the sea and the treacherous sands of the Qattara Depression.

This time our parting was full of hope, full of optimism, that soon we would be meeting again.

"They'll have to give us a rest and refit soon," he said with his familiar grin.

I watched him naked in the dawn. "Tooth not hurting?" I asked watching as he dressed for the drive back.

"Not a twinge," he smiled. He would not let me get up to see him off. "I'll take away the picture of you unclothed on the sheet, your face pink, hair all over the place on the pillow, the woman I've ravaged – the one I'm coming back to marry."

He came over to kiss me once more and quickly left the room.

Two days later he was dead.

Part Four

Chapter Nineteen

September in Tuscany, 1982.

I looked up from where I was reading and saw the man in the black beret who had so captured my interest. Despite the warm Italian air a shiver passed through my body.

For several days now I had eyed him across the dining-room of the Villa San d'Almazzo. He did not sit with us paying guests at the long refectory table, but at a small round one in a corner. With him were two others, both elderly, a man and a woman. He sat between them with his back to a French window. Though I could glimpse under the beret – apparently worn as perpetually as were the dark glasses – grizzled hair showing above his only visible ear, I thought he looked a good bit younger than his companions who were more likely to be in their eighties. It was difficult to gauge exactly the age of the man in the middle. His face was rugged in the extreme, skin like burnt sandpaper. He was probably in his mid-sixties though he could be older.

From my place at the big table I was able to unobtrusively watch the trio, and the more I watched the more I pondered upon them, particularly on the man in the beret who had a distinctive look – a man who, despite his obvious disabilities, carried with him a certain undefinable authority. The trio seemed to enjoy the good Italian fare, served by smiling maids, with plenty of excellent Chianti Classico from one of Tuscany's famous vineyards to wash it down. But, strangely enough, and in total contrast to the hubbub coming from our table, the three never appeared to address a word to one another.

"Who are they?" my curiosity got the better of me, and I enquired of Sister Catherine who was sitting in her office behind the glassed-in interior courtyard of the large rambling convent. "They never speak!"

"Over the years for sure they have said all there is to say," she replied in her soft Irish drawl; her unlined face a picture of tranquillity under the coif of her blue veil. "They are residents who live with us permanently," she continued. "Some keep to their rooms; some come up here for a change of air from our hospital for the destitute down in the city. The three you ask about are in a position to pay for their keep. We call them in-between cases, not bad enough to be hospitalized, yet needing supervision and care. "Signor Landi is stone deaf, the poor soul He has been a benefactor to the hospital for fifty years. Such a rare and devout man. His wife is . . ." she tapped her forehead suggestively.

"And the one who sits between them? What relation is he?" I queried.

"Oh, that one? No relation. That one's a miracle," Sister Catherine laughed. "During the last world war Italy was being fought over and there were many casualties; some of our nuns too. He was sent to us to die, but by the mercy o' God he did not die. His recovery was very slow. The Landis would visit him.

He was alone; no family. When he was well enough they took him to live with them in their *casa*."

"Was he able to work?" I did some quick calculations. The war had been forty years ago. He would probably have been a young man in his twenties then.

"Sure now, I believe he was. Light work for a semi-invalid, you understand . . . oh, excuse me," she stretched out a hand to take up the telephone ringing on her desk.

I thought about the man who so disturbed me. Saved by the nuns' devoted nursing and taken in by the kindness of the Landis until they were too incapacitated to look after him and themselves any more. The three then came to live in the haven of the Villa San d'Almazzo, situated above the tiny hamlet of that name. Here the 'miracle' man could be seen walking about the gardens, maybe with a stiff leg but with such a marvellously elegant bearing that every time I glimpsed him it brought a lump to my throat.

I left Sister Catherine coping with a long distance telephone booking, and walked out to the sun-drenched terrace with its palms and lemon trees and panoramic view of the red roofed city beyond San d'Almazzo village basking in the haze far below.

Though it was mid-September, it was still very hot in the sun, and I had taken to leaving my companions at the half-day mark after a morning's sightseeing followed by lunch in an open-air café. My friend Dulcie, leading our select group, had booked us into the convent which was less expensive than most hotels, and nicer if one wanted peace and quiet after the hussle of the crowds in the town. I say 'select' because Dulcie chose her small parties through personal recommendation of those genuinely interested, who wanted to learn in depth about art, and Florentine history in particular. I therefore should have been flattered when she asked me if I would like to join the forthcoming trip, but at first I had refused.

Our friendship had started from the time we met at a finishing school in Florence before the war. Afterwards we had kept in touch by sending each other Christmas cards. For years our ways had parted, until, on my husband's retirement, we went to live on her estate in Suffolk. I had married and had a family. Dulcie had not. She was more than ever a forceful character, an intellectual who besides writing books on the history of art, rode to hounds and was a magistrate. She had inherited the 'big house' on her father's death, had converted it, and lived in a spacious wing. We bought the stable block.

Dulcie could be very persuasive, and when I at first declined her offer to go to Italy, she told me in no uncertain terms that I had indulged enough in moping after a year of widowhood and that unless I wanted to become a permanent wet rag and a pain in the neck to my two sons and my friends, I had better snap out of it, and there was no more satisfactory way to do that than a holiday to revisit old haunts. "We might even have a look to see if our school is still there," she said.

"I am not half as interested in art as you are," I had protested. "You know I never furthered my studies in that line. I have hardly looked at a picture since those days and I can barely recall a word of Italian."

"*Ritorno*; it will come back. *Ritornello*, you may remember, can be translated as 'to be back in love

204

again'! Think of that! Even if you don't fall in love with Italy, I know you'll enjoy it. You needn't worry about a thing. I'll make all the arrangements."

I meekly agreed.

Three times the course of my life had been changed in a momentous way by my reluctantly agreeing to go somewhere I did not particularly wish to. The first was to a Ball when I was young and shy and trembling with nerves; the second was to do some voluntary work in the East End; the third time was now when I was over-persuaded to go to Italy when I would have much preferred to stay at home.

So it was therefore that in the early afternoons, after Dulcie had taken us round to some admittedly fascinating houses and crypts that no one else apparently had an *entré* to, and my ankles had swollen up in the heat, and I had been revived by a glass of wine with our daily pasta lunch under the shade of a pavement awning, I left the party and caught a bus back up to the hills. I descended from the bus stop down a steep slope and through the tall gates and along a drive to the convent. Here I collected a book from my 'cell' room and made my way to the old olive groves above the villa to put my feet up and read until tea time.

Afternoon tea was served by Sister Mary in the breakfast room punctually at four o'clock. Sister Mary, one of the ancient nuns on light duties – they never retired – could be quite stroppy if we were late in returning our cups from where we had wandered out onto the terraces.

"Is it not enough that I pour out your tea and give you a slice of cake baked in our kitchens? Do you expect me with my aching bunions to go all round the garden collecting the dirty crockery as well?" she would ask with pained voice if we were a minute over the five o'clock deadline imposed by her.

"Sorry Sister," I said straight-faced on a Sunday when Dulcie had taken the day off from conducting us. Earlier on we had been to Mass in the convent chapel. We exchanged glances and reverted to giggles at Sister Mary's indignant retreating form, rather as we used to behave when we were seventeen.

"You're better already," Dulcie observed, "though I am not so sure it is good for you to come back here to brood on your own."

"I don't brood," I said, "and I am not alone."

Chapter Twenty

But I did brood. After a morning of intensive viewing of art I needed the peace of the garden to digest and study my guidebook of the monuments and paintings seen that morning – or so I told myself. In reality I came back to watch the man in the beret taking his afternoon stroll during that quiet hour before tea-time.

Of course my interest had first been aroused by the headgear with its glint of a badge I could not distinguish. Frenchmen often wore berets, and so to a lesser degree did Italians. But those were small, flat affairs that fitted the head and were often of a dark navy colour. Why should an Italian gentleman (from his dress and table manners he was obviously no rough peasant) choose to wear a beret, a direct copy – even to the flap fold to the right side – of those distinctive ones of the Royal Tank Regiment I remembered from forty years ago?

The anguish I had suffered during the war had long been subjugated to the deep recesses of my mind and only now and then surfaced when something jogged my memory as was happening now. Why should I return early from my sightseeing to deliberately bring back memories best left buried? Why did I not change my place at table so that I could no longer look across at the man? What drew me like a magnet to the olive groves day after day to wait and watch for his figure once more?

Now I watched from my long chair the tall fragile-looking, excessively lean, grey-haired Italian with the beret walking the terraces in a slow deliberate manner that showed long familiarity with every stone or step or rise in the path before him; every now and then he would disappear from my sight behind a tree, round a corner or beneath a high oleander hedge in pink flower. Up the hillside he went and up again and round about and down a different way while my mind recalled those heady years before the war – and always the sickening knowledge of what happened later. And I damned the man I was watching. Damn all black berets to bring back such hurt, such emptiness, such stomach-churning pity for a young life lost.

Gough's last words to me still lay imprinted on my mind as if he had spoken them only yesterday.

Before leaving Egypt with John I saw Gough's grave outside the small casualty station where he had died. 'Mortally wounded' they reported. They did not say 'perished after a long day of agony'. Had he been conscious? I knew he had died on the evening of the day he had been wounded. A stray shell had hit him as darkness turned to light in the early morning when once again they were about to go into battle. When wounded at 5 a.m. he would have been incredibly brave; somehow he would have retained his humour. He had once told me he would refuse morphia. "While I am alive," he had said, "I want to be alive with all my faculties. Should I be killed – and, God, I've seen enough of my pals and my men being killed for the odds to make it my turn next – keep going for me won't you? We will meet again beloved whether in this world or in the next. Nothing can kill our love. Not partings – nor even death."

I had tried to trace one of the medical orderlies who had been with him. There were no nursing sisters up there so close to the front. But with the casualty station soon after overrun by Italians, I could find out nothing.

Nothing but some graves in a sandy waste with no indication to mark it as a burial place. There was a derelict nissen hut with one solitary post beside it and a few graves scattered in no particular order in a rocky, barren, pitted pittiless landscape. Gough's grave was heaped with stones into which a wooden cross had been fixed. On it was roughly painted in white the words: 'Major G.A.C. Nicholson, DSO and bar, MC Royal Tank Regiment. Aged 26.' And the date of his death – 14.7.42.

Someone had planted a bush at the base of the grave. Half uprooted by the bitter winds, it had long since died and the once-green leaves had turned into grey brittleness. It made me sick to look at it. The withered bush was trying to tell me that beneath the humped mound lay the decaying, shattered remains of the man I loved. It was impossible to believe that Gough's vivid personality with his abiding cheerfulness and abundance of courage could be lying in a sack rotting away under those merciless stones.

Later, much later, they removed the bodies from that small graveyard in the nothingless desert, and, placing them in coffins, reburied them with full military and religious honours in tidy white rows. They laid them in the new El Alamein War Cemetery, one kilometre along the old coastal road past the turning to the village, and 130 kilometres west of Alexandria which Gough with all the others had been the means of saving.

This ordered resting place, situated in the same forsaken desert, has an impressive arched entrance and a central cross. Beautifully tended, each similar headstone bears the individual's name and rank. For me it was too ordered, too regimental. In life Gough's tall figure would have stood out of any such ordered row! I preferred to think of him in the lonely heaped grave I had first seen.

But once I had read his name on a grave in the large, impersonal, dignified and so sad El Alamein War Cemetery, I accepted what I had known all along. Gough *was* truly dead.

I had left flowers there with a card on which I wrote:

'Lo, some we loved, the loveliest and the best.'

I never went back.

Chapter Twenty-One

Now, from my chair, and all these years later, I watched with resentment the man who brought back the past so poignantly. I told myself I need not have gone there to sit with my feet up on the chair extension, my guidebook in my lap, and watch the figure moving through the paths in the shady groves. I could have been down with the others at the Pitti Palace or the Uffizi, or walking once again over the lovely Ponte Vecchio bridge which neither the Allies nor Germans had bombed but had by mutual agreement left intact.

Yet, instead of being with my party, here I was watching the man in the black beret coming nearer. Each foot was placed carefully, almost toe slithered and followed by a slight hesitation as bandsmen do when marching to slow music. He was dressed in an impeccable white suit with waistcoat, shirt and dark tie – and the beret worn at that extreme angle, the right side exaggeratedly low so that it covered his ear and half his cheek. This overlap did little to shade his face from the sun. If he wanted shade why did he not wear a panama hat – such as his deaf benefactor wore when out shuffling along on the arm of one of the nursing nuns – a hat which anyway would have gone better with his posh suiting and spotless white shoes? With every step that brought the Italian nearer to where I sat, I boiled with resentment for the beret he usurped.

As the gap between us closed I noticed that the foot-rest on the chair where I reclined jutted out a little over the path. I put down my book, swept my feet over to one side of the chair, and stood up. The sound of my rising caught his attention and he came to a halt. Scraping back my chair a couple of feet I said in my rusty Italian, "*Scusa*, my chair was in your path."

There was a pause while I stared at the man come to stand stock still not a yard away from me. Was he staring back at me through those dark glasses? He seemed to be though again I could not tell. It was the first time I had seen him close to, and my eyes were rivetted on the silver cap badge which I had only seen before as a glint in the distance.

It was, unmistakably, the regimental badge of the Royal Tank Corps, worn since its formation in 1923. On the badge and topping it was a crown, below which a garland laurel wreath encircled a central tank seen sideways on. The regimental motto 'Fear Naught' was emblazoned beneath. I held my breath in disbelief. I felt I could not very well at a first encounter bluntly ask the *signor* how he had come by the beret with its badge. Perhaps he had served with the British forces? Could be. Or with the partisans against Mussolini? There was an awful mix-up at that time when there was a cease-fire with the Italians but not with the Germans.

Then, "*Grazie, signorna*," the man said.

Before I could collect my wits as to how to ask the question which so intrigued me, the man lifted a hand to his head in a semi-salute and passed on his way.

For a long while I stood rooted to the ground staring after him. The words '*grazie signora*' had come out in perfect Italian but slowly and somewhat slurred as a drunk might speak. Yet instinctively I knew that the man was not drunk. Moreover I knew from Aunt Dora's illness that the slur could indicate a stroke. I had noticed too that one of his arms hung down loosely straight.

However, what stunned me of course was the cap badge. It was so familiar. I collapsed onto my long chair and lay staring out unseeing at the view. A whole pandora's box of memories continued to assail me.

'*Ritornello*', Dulcie had said. Ah yes, *ritornello* indeed. I was back again in those days when I was in love . . .

Chapter Twenty-Two

With a start I awoke to find myself in my small convent cell-room with the crucifix on the wall above my bed. I had hardly slept. Throughout the night I had recalled the vivid details of my younger days, memories brought on by my encounter with the Italian wearing the black beret. The nostalgia I felt was for the far past and also for John whom I had lost only a year ago.

It was John who had broken the news to me in Cairo. I do not think I could have got through those first weeks if it had not been for him. The initial reports that had come through to GHQ Cairo, were that Gough had been wounded; I had every hope. It was therefore all the more terrible when John told me as gently as he could that the wounds had proved fatal.

I had to cable Babs, poor Babs; they had all gone now – all her family.

Letters poured in. Gough's General at Advanced GHQ wrote how he had not wished to lose him. He was as brilliant a Staff Officer as he was a fighting man. But Gough had wanted to go where he was badly needed to lead and restore morale. Frank wrote that the RTR Gough had joined was a good Tank Regiment: 'One of the best. It was he who lifted and inspired them to win. Not one of them would have seen him killed if by laying down his life he could have prevented it. Your Gough was a brilliant young soldier whom none of us who knew him will ever forget and whose influence and example will always remain an inspiration'.

'Gough was the personification of all we stand for,' wrote another. 'I for one always felt better for having been with him'. 'Without Gough's inspiring leadership', wrote 'Blood', Gough's old commander at Beda Fomm, 'we should never have stopped the Italians as we did'.

After sometime came the official version of what had happened sent by an officer on the spot in the Royal Horse Artillery:

. . . At 1600 hrs Major Gough Nicholson of the 6 RTR, arrived with orders. He is Officer Commanding our column which consists of 16 'Honey' tanks, a troop of armoured cars from the Royals as well as our Battery RHA. Tomorrow morning the 9th Australian Division which has just returned to the desert from Syria, is attacking the El Daba aerodrome astride the main road. If they capture their objective, which is hoped will be the case by 0900 or 1000 hrs, then this column will go through them. The duration of the party is expected to be about 36 hours.

At 1630 hrs we moved north across the railway by Imayid station and had the evening brew alongside the main road 3 to 4 miles to the west of that station.

. . . At 0030 hrs we moved west down the main road with Major Gough Nicholson leading the way, tanks in front of us. It was 0230 hrs before we settled for the night just north of the main road and in front of the Australian guns as ordered. The Australian attack was timed to start at 0330 hrs.

At 0530 hrs, daylight, we dispersed. The Brigade Commander and OC Column were standing beside the leading tank from which the latter, Major Nicholson, had just descended. They were consulting together and viewing the scene through their binoculars when the first 105 shell of the morning wounded both officers, the OC Column so badly that he died that evening at the nearest Field Casualty Station. During that night the Field Station was overrun by the Italians who evacuated the wounded prisoners to further behind the lines for shipment to Italy. On the retaking of the Field Station by the British the next day, the Allied dead were buried nearby.

Later it was learnt that the enemy only had one Troop of 105s on this particular front, the remainder being A/T guns. The Troop was captured by the Australians after firing only 9 rounds. The sortie was successfully accomplished within the time allotted. (End of Official War Diary).

When I read the report I was physically sick. It seemed too cruel. Not killed in the thick of battle but standing by his tank in consultation with the Brigadier while waiting to go into action. A one off shell – the first of only a few rounds. It could have landed harmlessly anywhere in the desert at that range.

To add to my total misery I continued to be sick. In my acute distress it took me some time to realize that this was not just due to shock and sadness, but that I was pregnant. With the knowledge that within me I had Gough's child, I began to live again.

John and I were married as soon as possible – Gough would not have wanted his offspring to be born out of wedlock, and John said the baby needed to have a father, and he would be honoured to help bring up the child of a man so highly thought of, one who had given his life for his country. We did not sleep together until after the baby's birth. Under two years later John's own son was born.

We told no one at first that the eldest boy was not John's – that is except for Babs.

I told Babs. I had gone up to Scotland to be with her and Angus and the two children for a week when she was dying of cancer. She said she had already guessed. She said that Gough had always loved me. Even in those years when he could not find me he had never looked at another girl.

Angus died in the seventies. Their children are delightful. The girl is a lovely red-head, and the boy is tall and athletic like all the Nicholsons.

Chapter Twenty-Three

Later on the day after my near sleepless night, and after pulling out early as usual from my sightseeing with Dulcie, I composed myself on the chaise-longue in the same place as before on one of the lower terraces. There was a table beside me, and next to the table an upright chair.

When I saw the Italian taking his usual walk before tea-time on the terraces above me I made my way into the breakfast room a little earlier than usual, collected a tray, and asked for two cups of tea and a plate with two slices of cake. Sister Mary looked at me curiously when I said one cup was for the Italian gentleman in the black beret, and would she pour it as he liked it, please. She said nothing as she poured out the tea. I assuaged her curiosity by saying I wanted to ask the *Signor* about the British badge on his beret. She nodded and handed me the tray.

I rose to meet the Italian on the path as he came my way. "I have a tray here with refreshments, *Signor*," I said in English. "Will you join me?"

He seemed slightly taken aback but nevertheless accepted courteously. I indicated the chair with my hand. Quietly he made his way past my chair and the table.

"Sister Mary has poured your tea as you like it," I

continued, putting cup and plate out. We were still standing beside our chairs.

"May I introduce myself? I am Isabella Shawe. I am here with friends for the sightseeing and to recover after my husband's death."

"My sincere condolences, *Signora*. A beautiful name – Isabella. Italian, I think?"

"They say Huguenot."

"Signor Dāvid Landi," he said with a slight bow. He pronounced it Daveed, the Italian way. So, he had taken on the name of his benefactors, the Landis.

"Please do sit down. It must be difficult for you; I mean getting around."

"I am used to it. I am told I do not exercise enough; that I am lazy. It is true. I do not make the effort."

"But you walk so well, and you speak excellent English."

He smiled at the compliment, a rather sweet one-sided smile from full lips. "English came to me more easily than the Italian. When I regained consciousness in hospital after my wounding – in the war you understand, *Signora* – I had to learn everything: to speak; to understand – everything. I was like a newborn baby with no past but oh, with such pain. I think babies suffer. They too cannot speak. Only I was not a baby. I was a man with a hole in my head."

"You hide the wound very well under the beret, *Signor*," I praised. "Tell me, how did you meet the Landis?"

"In the hospital. They are good people, always helping others. They visited those of us who had no families, prisoners-of-war too, bringing us choco-lates, fruit and cigarettes. After I was discharged they

219

took me to live with them in their villa above here. They gave me their name. I was a young man then, a young man shattered by war." He sighed. "The years have gone quickly and comfortably due to the Signor and Signora Landi. They urged me to take an interest in the famous pictures below. I sat and copied them and learnt in this way to paint myself. It is little to have accomplished in forty years."

"Do you talk with the other guests, make friends?"

"Not possible. Signora Landi's mind has gone, and the Signor is too deaf for conversation. Besides, people do not like to look at me. I see them look, and then look away, and afterwards they avoid me. It is unpleasant. I prefer to keep to myself. When they took the bandages off they gave me a mirror. It was terrible. I did not even know what I had looked like before to compare. I knew what I felt, but the face looking back at me was nothing to do with me. I was a lost person. I wanted to hide from the world. I am used to it now. I keep away. I do not speak to children for fear that I frighten them."

"You do not frighten me," I said slowly and thought how sad not to be able to speak to children. "I have seen people scarred by bombing and war." He had been well looked after, kept in cotton wool by the nuns and Signora Landi who was now senile. It seemed to me that this Italian immaculately dressed in his white had been perhaps too cosseted for too long. He needed outside interests, see other places . . .

"I hope you do not think it impertinent of me to ask personal questions?" The last thing I wanted to do was to put my foot in it and alienate the man who so intrigued me.

"I am honoured, *Signora*," he replied chivalrously. "It is not often that an English lady of goodness and distinction bothers to ask questions of an old half-witted fellow."

Aha, I thought to myself again, remembering the days when I was being 'finished' in Florence; Italians. Flatterers all. But how charming! "You are far from being half-witted," I protested.

"My brain," he said dryly indicating his head, "it does not always work well." Did I detect irony there? A glimpse of humour. Like Gough? He was so like Gough might have grown old, thinner perhaps, but still a very tall man and still with that upright braced-back stature of one who had been a soldier. And this man *had* been a soldier if only a war-time one. If Gough had been so wounded and had not died would he have lost his sparkle, his interest in people and the life all about him? But then Gough would have had myself, Babs and innumerable friends to tell him about himself had he lost his memory. It was a terrible thing that this man here had found no relations, no friends, no one to tell him about himself. Why, as an Italian, had not someone who had known him in his country not come forward? A mother, sister, father would have recognized him in hospital even if half his head was blown away. Could they not have advertised? It did not make sense to me.

"May I enquire if you have travelled?" I tried another tactic after a pause during which I sipped my tea pensively.

"*Si*, in Italy with the *Signor* and *Signora*. To France once and also to Greece. I love the sea. You live in England, London? I would like to see England.

I have dreams, so many dreams of where I do not know."

"What sort of dreams?"

"Of boats on the sea, of green fields and the voices of children laughing. Of a mother," he said softly, "brothers and sisters. I must have had a family. I must have come from somewhere."

"The beret you wear," I began slowly the subject that had first interested me, "it intrigues me, especially the badge. Do you know what the badge is?"

"*Si*. I know. The Tommy in the hospital told"

"*Scusa*," I interrupted. "What hospital? Where?"

"Caserta."

"Caserta?" I gasped, "that was where there was a large British prisoner-of-war camp was it not?"

"I was told so. I only knew the hospital. My first conscious memory is a ward of beds with other badly wounded like myself."

"What nationalities?"

"All nationalities," he shrugged. "Italians, English, Australians, South Africans – only those on the dangerously ill list, you understand. We were all there together. There was an Englishman in the bed beside me. They call all English soldiers 'Tommy' in my country. For a long time I could not speak but I could hear him talking to his 'mate' on the other side. I could see a little with the one eye, and I could hear very well with the undamaged ear. I took in more than they knew because of not being able to speak. When the 'mate' was moved, the Englishman talked to me incessantly. I did not want to listen to him; I wished he would stop, but on and on he went driving me mad. Signor Landi said the man saved my life by talking and stopping me drifting off into many

222

unconscious periods. After a while I began to form the English words with my mouth and the sounds came out. The boy was so pleased! It was he who taught me to speak English."

"After all, I suppose you had plenty of time lying there."

"*Si*, it was a long long time we were in the beds next to one another. I had nothing in my locker except what the Landis brought me, but the Englishman had one or two things. He had his identity disc on a string, his cap with silver tank badge. Before he died he gave me the beret. He said it was all he had to give away and he wanted me to have it. He said to wear it. He said, 'it will cover your hole!' When he died I cried. I kept the beret under my pillow and would not be parted from it. I cried for the English boy who had nagged and nagged at me and made me talk. He was my first friend in the new world."

"He told you he was in the Royal Tank Corps? Was he wounded in Italy?"

"He was wounded in Africa and shipped over. A nightmare journey he told. Many died on the way. They were short of doctors and nurses. The Englishman's death affected me badly. I wanted to die too."

"What happened next?"

"I do not remember much. I was very ill and expected not to recover. The *Signor* took special interest in my case at this time when Italy was in turmoil. He arranged for me to be taken by private ambulance to the Little Sister's Hospital for the Dying in Florence, one affiliated to this convalescent convent where, as you know, for some years now they take in tourists and students as paying guests which helps to raise money for the hospital. The nuns are the dedicated Blue-veiled Irish nurses. I clutched the beret all the way in the ambulance."

"And you did not die. You got better. The nuns here told me you are their miracle man."

"*They* are the miracle workers! No, I did not die, the Good God only knows why for I had no wish to live as a cripple without even a name. I perfected my English with the nuns though of course they all speak Italian, and the Landis too are bilingual."

"So, how at last did you come to wear the beret?"

He smiled, that sweet smile; I was almost looking for Gough's dimple, but this man's face was too thin for one. "When the bandages were taken off they brought me a mirror. There was such a raw mess of holes and red criss-cross puckerings that I did not see how I could ever face the world. I wished I *had* died. I was a monster. Then I remembered the English Tommy's words and the beret. I put it on. Well, it covered the worst up. The nuns all gathered round in my ward. They said how well it suited me. I looked in the mirror and felt perhaps I could go outside with it on. I have worn it continuously since. Not the original you understand. They become soiled and they get sent to the cleaners, like a wig in the old times! I like to wear the badge in memory of the brave Englishman."

"Was there a name-tag in the original beret, the name of the Tomnmy?"

"Only the name of the makers in London. I can order them direct but they copy them well enough in the city."

"You put the beret on correctly, I mean at the correct angle. How did you come to do this?"

"Correctly?" he queried with a puzzled frown. "How correctly? I put it on, that is all."

"You see," I murmured, "I once knew a man who wore the black beret . . ." I thought, as I was speaking, how extraordinary. Was it instinct the way he . . .? Could he have been in the Tank Corps without knowing it?

"You can tell me about this man? You can tell me about Tommy?" he said eagerly sitting forward in his chair.

"No, not him I'm afraid. Another man who wore a similar beret. I'll tell you about him another day." I glanced at my watch. "Oh, good heavens, just look at the time," I exclaimed. "Gone five o'clock. Sister Mary will be after me!" I picked up the tray ready to take it back to the convent.

"I continue my walk," Signor Dāvid Landi rose carefully to his tall height. "Please *Signora*, we meet again? I have enjoyed our little talk."

"I too," I replied with truth. "Tomorrow? Join me for tea here again tomorrow."

I walked down the path with the tray in my hands and with my mind racing.

Chapter Twenty-Four

The next morning at breakfast I told Dulcie I would not be going down to the city with them that day.

"What's going on?" she asked. "You've already missed enough surely, and we've only got ten days to go. There is so much to examine and study."

"I'm sure, Dulcie," I said. "I've enjoyed the trip immensely and I've learnt a lot about art. You must believe me it's marvellous how interesting you make it all, but . . ."

"But what? Who is this man in the black beret who seems to mesmerize you?"

"He wears the cap badge of the Royal Tank Regiment."

"Same as Gough? Oh, come off it Bel. That's all so long ago. There must be thousands and thousands of tank badges lying around all over the place."

Dulcie had never met Gough but she knew quite a bit about him: that we had fallen in love; that we had been engaged; that I had gone out to Cairo to marry him; that before we could be he had been killed. She knew John, of course, both when she was in London in the early days and later when John retired and we bought her stables.

"I know," I said again, "plenty of badges lying about. I want to find out more about him and time is short. The funny part is he's not unlike what Gough might have grown to look like with age."

"Don't be daft," laughed Dulcie. She went into the dark hall to gather her party together, while I made my way to Sister Catherine sitting in her office in the glassed-in interior of the courtyard.

"Have you a moment, Sister? May I have a word with you?"

"Of course, Mrs Shawe. Please take a chair," she said in her pleasant lilt. "What can I do for you?"

I came straight to the point. "Could you arrange for me to have a talk with the elder Signor Landi? It is about the cap badge which the younger *Signor* wears on his beret. I can assure you this is not just curiosity on my part but genuine interest. Before and during the last conflict I worked in the War Office in London and had much to do with men in the Tank Corps. The *Signor* tells me it was given to him by a British soldier in hospital. The elder Signor Landi may be able to tell me more about the man."

"By all means. I'm sure he would be glad to help. As you know he is deaf and now quite ill with an ageing disease. A nurse attends him and his wife. I suggest you talk in the garden away from others. You will have to shout," she added with a twinkle.

"Where and when would it be convenient, Sister?"

"On one of the lower terraces where he takes an airing. After twelve noon would be best. I will tell him to expect you."

I found him there, and with the nurse on one side and me on the other we started a screaming match. The elder Signor Landi was a man of means; a devout Roman Catholic and instigator of several philanthropic and charitable ventures, in particular the hospital for the destitute and the dying in the city below. I said I was interested in the Signor Dāvid Landi; he reminded me of an Englishman I had known who had been killed in the war in North Africa.

"Killed in the war. An Englishman, looks like Signor Dāvid," shouted the Irish nurse from along the bench.

"Could Signor Dāvid have been a British prisoner-of-war?" I yelled.

"Who knows?" the old man shouted back equally loudly, presumably because otherwise he could not hear his own voice. "At one time I wondered. He is very tall for an Italian. Also he picked up English more quickly than he did our language. Remarkable with the brain damage he suffered that he could learn two languages. All memory of before gone, alas."

The conversation went on, much of it repeated by the nurse in a sort of loud echo to what I said.

"He was a mystery right from the start and has remained so," the old man continued. "It is a tragedy. He came to Caserta at the same time as the British Tommy in a draft of seriously wounded. Conditions were very bad in the base hospitals of Tripoli and Tunis where the wounded were collected. Many died. Many more succumbed on the sea transport from Africa. There were several dangerously ill prisoners-of-war with our men, the young Tommy among them.

"I first saw Dāvid in September 1942 at Caserta. He was about six weeks in deep unaware before regaining periods of consciousness greatly due to the Tommy.

228

I found the case interesting. Something exceptional about him touched me. Despite his terrible wounds I could see he was a fine figure of a man, dark-haired like Italians, but not so dark. His skin was of a lighter colour burnt ruddy by the sun; not deep brown like most.

"I went to the matron and surgeons of the hospital and to the Commandant of the Prisoner-of-War Camp in Caserta where the not so ill were interned. He was a puzzle to them also. Later they received the missing lists from England and Germany. Dāvid did not fit into any of those either. Had he been British he would have been one of the nine hundred repatriated to the United Kingdom in exchange for an equal number of our PoWs on the seriously ill list who would never fight again. The exchange took place in neutral Spain. The wounded were carried aboard a Swedish ship, also neutral."

I did not say I knew about who was neutral and who was not. I was finding it an extremely tiring and inconclusive conversation.

"What happened next?" was all I said.

"The Germans were being pushed up through Italy by the Americans and British. Our country was in turmoil, a battlefield fought over by two foreign armies. At that time we had two Italian governments as well as two armies of our own and many groups of partisans. In this desperate situation the hospitals were being evacuated. I would not let them take Dāvid. A journey then by army ambulance convoy would have killed him. The roads were in turmoil in those days when Mussolini fell. It was a time impossible in which to investigate further with thousands of British PoWs escaping from camps. Believe me Senor Dāvid was not the only lost one.

"We resolved to take him with us privately and put him in my hospital with the nuns where at least he could die in a dignified manner. But he lived and we took him home with us. We called him Dāvid after Michelangelo's statue in our city, because he has the same fine bearing and good figure. He became like a son to us and now we are old we worry for him. The nuns will look after him but without us he will stagnate mentally and go into one of his troughs. He needs stimulation, an interest in life. After all he is not yet an old man."

"He told me he paints."

"We think he is talented. He has let the art go since we came to the convent to live. He needs the studio in our *casa* to work in."

"You let your home?"

"*Si*, for six months. We hoped to go back, but with my wife's illness and my difficulties the hope has faded. We thought it better Dāvid should be with us, but he misses the studio with the beautiful view where he spent hours happy at his painting."

I was exhausted with shouting and I think I had exhausted Signor Landi too, as well as the nurse! I thanked him for his kindness in giving me of his time, and he said *de riente*, it was nothing, and that he hoped I would kindly continue to talk to Dāvid while I was here.

Now I no longer accompanied Dulcie and our group but met Dāvid morning and afternoon. Sometimes we just sat and talked on one of the terraces, at other times we walked through the gardens. Soon

I suggested we go further: up the drive from the convent and down to the village and then back round the other way. On these excursions I made him take my arm for I was afraid he might stumble and fall.

"I do not need to," he protested huffily, the first time, "I can see where my feet are going well enough." He soon relented with, "I do not wish to seem ungracious. It is very pleasant to take the lady Isabella's arm!" I glimpsed the humour again. Would I ever get him to laugh?

The difference in our heights seemed to me to be much the same as it had been with Gough. Perhaps I too had shrunk an inch or so with age. At any rate I enjoyed the walks arm in arm with this tall statuesque man.

He asked me why I was so interested in the Tank badge, and I told him that I had once had a boyfriend in that Corps of the army, a man called Gough Nicholson who was also very tall; one who was devoted to tanks. I went on to say that we had become engaged but before we could be married he had been killed in North Africa.

"That is sad. So much suffering in war, and for the women. Please to tell me more, Signora Isabella, about this man Gough."

I did. In the end I told him most things – all the way from how we had first met at a Ball, to my life in London with my aunt, and how after her death he and his sister invited me to their home in Dorset and I became one of the family. In an extraordinary way, as I related the story, Dāvid seemed to me to take on the mantle of Gough, a Gough wounded in the head whom I was reminding of things that he could not remember, so much so that I began to think of him as

231

English. And it was not just me. Dāvid was fascinated by Gough's story, a man who had been killed in the desert by a shell at much the same period he had been wounded in heaven knew where.

At one time when we were resting from a steep climb up a hill to a small chapel where there was a magnificent panorama of the plain below stretching away at our feet, I asked Dāvid if he would take off his dark glasses.

"I look ugly," he said still hiding from the world behind them and the beret.

"I have seen wounds before in the Blitz on London," I replied gently. "It is just as well to know."

Reluctantly he took off the spectacles and pushed the flap of the beret a little aside. There was a black patch over the empty socket, but the other eye looked at me, blinking a little in the unaccustomed bright light, but steadily enough. It was a brown eye, a kindly one, the eyebrow above it dark brown.

"Seen enough?" Dāvid smiled at me, the corner of the eye wrinkling up. The thick grey hair above his ear curled in the same endearing way Gough's had, moreover the one visible ear was not entirely flat to his head but stuck out a mite to make him look boyishly young for a grey head.

What little I could see of the scar was indeed terrible: a great hole in the head with a sort of tin plate pinned in it. There was no ear lobe or surround and the skin on temple and down cheek was puckered, red, and terribly disfigured even after all these years. Since they had 'patched him up' in the original hospital, plastic surgery had come on in leaps and bounds. I was sure there was a great

232

deal more they could do nowadays to match the undamaged side of his face.

I did not express these thoughts then – after all it was none of my business and Dāvid may have already refused any more medication for all I knew. But I did say as he put on his dark glasses and pulled the beret firmly down to cover much of his cheek again, "You are *so* like Gough it is unbelievable."

He laughed then, a deep throaty unaccustomed laugh. "I think I shall take on this mantle of your Gough for my past!" he expressed with more exuberance in his voice than I had heard before. Smiling I took his arm and we resumed our walk. "I like this man," he continued. "I like his family. I would like to see where he lived and where the British tanks are."

"One day, why not?" I said.

Chapter Twenty-Five

Then everything began to happen at once. I was sitting at one of the round tables on the terrace under the vine waiting for Dāvid to come out and join me for morning coffee when, to the consternation of myself and the other guests, Signora Landi suddenly appeared in the doorway stark naked, her grey tangled hair hanging down her back. She began to prance round the tables in a lewd and macabre dance while she sang high-pitched some Neopolitan love song. There was a moment of total disbelief while we all gasped in horror. I thanked God that neither her husband nor Dāvid were there to see her. Then one of the nuns came rushing out with a blanket to cover the poor deranged woman. The nun lead her away, still singing, to her room.

After that Signora Landi had a nurse in attendance night and day. She never left her room above the courtyard. Sometimes we would see her standing by the open window making faces and singing her weird songs.

"I've decided not to return with you," I informed Dulcie on the day before our scheduled departure.

"You're as mad as Signora Landi," Dulcie frowned. "What about your home, your sons, grandchildren, the work you do for the Red Cross, the visiting, the tennis, golf and bridge? You're not giving all that up for a whim?"

"I haven't said I am," I tossed my head huffily. "I'll be back. But I feel I need to stay on here for the moment."

"You can't be serious about Signor Landi?"

"What do you think of him – objectively?" I countered.

"Well, I grant you, his face in profile is very handsome. He has a good figure for a man of his age. On the other hand he is slow, his speech is slurred, he is a semi-invalid who needs looking after. Also he'd be an expensive undertaking. He must have an enormous bill from cleaners for those immaculate white suits! You nursed John in his last illness for long enough in all conscience. For goodness sake, Bel, you don't want to tie yourself down with another invalid."

"*Dulcie*, do stop jumping to conclusions. There is no question of my taking anyone on. Besides I don't suppose he . . . I'm intrigued by him that's all, especially about his past which remains a mystery. I just want to go on ferreting for a bit longer. I'll come back soon I promise you."

Dulcie said she would keep an eye on my stable block, and I gave her letters to post at home to the boys saying I was extending my holiday. Autumn was a lovely time to be in Italy. The weather was cooling down nicely. It really had been terribly hot until now . . .

After Dulcie and her party left, the elder Signor Landi asked me to join their table in the place of his poor wife. I accepted with alacrity. By this time I simply could not see enough of Dāvid. The man fascinated me, chiefly through his tall bearing unbowed by adversity. I kept on thinking that was exactly how Gough would have coped with and greatly overcome such a disaster. Besides he was *so like* him: soft brown of eye; deep of voice; artistic long-fingered hands – hands that . . . *Could* there have been a mistake over the burial? *Was* this man Gough? I wanted to watch Dāvid, to discover all I could find out. Then I would go home and do some research.

In the meantime Dāvid and I spent every day together. We talked of his life with the Landis. We talked of the past; my past. There was soon little that Dāvid did not know about the Nicholsons and about Gough, not to mention my life. I was interested that some time ago he had enjoyed sailing in Greece on a cruise with other disabled people. "Did you swim?" I asked.

"No, I have not swum. The arm and leg are too weak, you understand?"

"Did you not have swimming therapy? They say the exercise in water is particularly beneficient to develop wasted muscles."

"I have not done any since I left hospital. I do daily exercises in my room."

"When did you leave hospital?"

"1950. I started to know life again in the autumn of 1942. I was eight years in hospital."

"Eight years," I repeated with a lump in my throat. "Oh Dāvid, eight years . . ."

When I told him I had to go back to England he showed his distress. He took off his dark glasses and looked at me sadly. "I will miss you, Isabella," he said.

"I too will miss you," I answered. "I have my family in England as you know. But I will come back, I promise."

I promised the nuns too. "You have given the *Signor* new hope; rejuvenated our miracle man," Sister Catherine chirruped. "He has a new spring to his step, and is healthier for all the walks."

"Who now will return the cups of tea on time?" grumbled old Sister Mary. "Signor Landi won't that's for sure."

I went back to my converted stables. Once again I was alone in the house. I missed John not being there, but I was too busy with my new preoccupation to mourn any more. My sons and daughters-in-law came to see me bringing my grandchildren, each child with a different character, all lovely in my doting eyes! We had fun and there was much laughter in the house but I did not mention the man in the black beret. With hidden eyes I re-examined my eldest son now forty years old. He had the same brown eyes, the same thick hair that was straight on top though it was fairer, the same marvellous figure as Gough – as Dāvid. Gough and Dāvid. Could Dāvid . . .? I set about finding more.

First I went to the old War Office, now the Ministry of Defence, to investigate the evidence of Major Gough Nicholson's death. I was sent to another department where files were brought out. There was nothing more in them than what I already knew. There was the War Diary, of which I had a copy, on what had happened in the early morning of that fatal day as Gough was about to go into action. There was a statement that the two wounded officers had been rushed off to the nearest Field Station at El Imayid by the railway line they had crossed to position themselves for the assault on El Daba aerodrome. It was from here that the air attacks were being such a nuisance to the Allies. At the Field Station, the Brigadier, less severely wounded than the Major, had been taken to a hospital some distance away by ambulance. Major Nicholson was considered too dangerously ill to be moved. The time of Major Nicholson's death was not recorded due to the casualty station having been overrun by the Italians that night. There was no record of an exact time. The Italians occupied it temporarily and took prisoner the staff and wounded. They then evacuated the place, leaving the dead.

"Could there have been a mix-up over bodies when the British came back and buried their dead?" I asked the sergeant in charge of the records. "Could one of them have been *thought* to be Major Nicholson when in fact he was still alive and had been taken prisoner? You see he did not die instantly. He was wounded at 5 a.m. and was reported to have lived throughout that day."

"Unlikely to have been a mix-up," the sergeant replied, "there must have been evidence on the body of rank, Tank regiment and decorations for it to have been written on the wooden cross."

"But his papers could have been left behind on another casualty, could they not?" I persisted.

"The only way to discover if it is the right or wrong officer is to have the body exhumed, dental records, et cetera, checked. The body, I understand, was later transferred to the El Alamein Cemetery. Exhumation can only take place in very exceptional circumstances, and you, Madam, would have to provide a great deal more evidence, plus permission from next of kin before the process could be acted upon. May I enquire who the next of kin are?"

"Major Nicholson's nephew and niece, I suppose. I don't think they'd be interested. His parents, his brother and sister, have all died."

"Forty years is a long time, Madam."

Once again, after all those years, I felt the sergeant was looking at me as if I, a mere fiancée, really had no business . . . I could see he was curious. "Of course," he added "should the Major after all be found to be alive there would be quite a fortune in pension due to him."

The insinuation was there in his voice. It was not pleasant, and I ended the interview by haughtily saying I would be obliged if he would investigate further to find if there was anyone alive – doctor, orderly, wounded, patient or whatever – who had been there at the time and could throw some light on the then situation.

I left knowing he would do the minimum. I then tried the Commonwealth War Graves Commission in Maidenhead to find out if I could gather any information on the body when it was moved to the El Alamein Cemetery.

They were more helpful there and not so suspicious of my investigation. Apparently on exhumation from its shroud there was found no identification on the body which had been badly damaged down one side by a shell. I already knew from reports sent to Cairo at the time that the identity disc Gough had been

239

wearing had been blasted away without trace as had most of his clothes with the contents of his pockets.

It occurred to me that the inscription on the cross could have easily been wired through from GHQ in Cairo. An officer known to Gough must have attended the burial and given the instructions for the cross. He could well have been the one who had planted the bush seen in the photograph I had been sent, and then seen for myself.

There was no further evidence to be found at the War Graves Commission. The macabre investigation was making me quite ill. I plodded on, determined to uncover every stone I could.

Next I went to Bovington. Once again they had nothing to suggest that Gough had not died of his wounds on the date recorded, nor that the body could have been another soldier's mistakenly interred in Gough's name.

"What makes you think there might have been a mistake, Mrs Shawe?" the Director of the Tank Museum and Archives asked.

"Only that there is a wounded ex-soldier of about the right age in Italy who looks extraordinarily like Major Nicholson, or rather as I imagine he might have grown old."

"Have you asked this man his name?"

"He has a severe head wound and other disabilities similar to those reported to have killed Major Nicholson. He cannot remember who he is or anything at all before coming to in a hospital in Caserta. He had no identification on him. There were some severely wounded British prisoner-of-war patients with him among the Italians, all badly wounded. One other-ranker gave the unknown man a Tank beret complete with badge before he died. He gave it to help cover up the head wound once the bandages had been removed. The man had to learn to talk and walk again. To this day he cannot recall his name or background or even his nationality. He did not fit in with any in the British 'missing' category. In the hospital they seemed to take it for granted he was Italian . . ." I ended lamely, seeing the expression of incredulity on the face of my interrogator.

"Humm," the Director cleared his throat. "I am sorry, Mrs Shawe, we really cannot help you here."

However, I *was* invited to see Gough's decorations which Babs had donated to the Museum after the war. I browsed through *The Tank* magazines during Gough's time, and the War Diaries which mentioned him in various actions, and I found out about two more awards. The first was a Mention-in-Despatches for his stand in an awkward situation at a place called Mechili in late January 1941 after Tobruk had been taken by the British and before the brilliant campaign when Gough had been awarded the DSO at Beda Fomm. The second Mentioned-in-Despatches was awarded posthumously for his routing of one of Rommel's units in the desert at El Alamein on 9th July 1942. I remembered clearly Gough's description of this battle in his last letter to me, when he wrote they had 'knocked spots off the Germans and chased them for miles'. I was glad to know he had been recognized for that 'glorious romp' when 'tails were high', and he was filled with hope for victory in the near future.

There were a few more venues worth trying. Signor Landi had told me that Dāvid's blood group was O Rhesus Positive. I now discovered in the files on Gough that his was the same. That these two were of a similar blood group proved nothing at all! I wondered if I should try and find out Gough's dentist's address and enquire about his records to compare with Dāvid's, though I felt this would be rather impertinent of me. I decided it was not worth the hassle and trouble for the small amount of evidence it might produce. Dāvid's jaw had been badly smashed on the one side. The dental surgeon in Florence had done an excellent crown job in rebuilding and capping new teeth on the roots of the old. The bridgework would scarcely resemble the old.

I searched my mind for what else I could do to prove or disprove that Signor Dāvid Landi was or was not Gough Nicholson. I thought it wiser not to tell my immediate family what I was doing, and I had received nothing but sceptical looks and no encouragement whatsoever to persevere from those I approached officially.

In John I had lost a very dear husband, and then out of the blue, in an extraordinary way it seemed to me, Gough had turned up again. I desperately wanted Dāvid to be Gough, yet every way I turned I came up against a brick wall.

Even handwriting let me down. While I was in England Dāvid and I corresponded. He was right handed as Gough had been, but due to the paralysis on that side he had learnt to write left handed which writing was rounded, awkward and rather childish-looking. It was nothing like Gough's firm clear neat handwriting I knew so well from all his letters. Would Dāvid's have been similar to Gough's had he been able to write right-handed now?

I did not know and never would know. I had

no concrete evidence whatsoever. Also I did not think it right for me to drag Dāvid into all sorts of interrogations and medical tests that might be traumatic for him and open up the pain he had suffered. What I did know was when I was beaten, and I gave up all idea of more investigations.

But nothing would stop me from watching him and noticing and wondering . . .

Chapter Twenty-Six

A telephone call came from Sister Catherine to say old Signor Landi had had a massive stroke and died. The Signor Dāvid was devastated. They were worried about him. Could I come immediately?

I was there by the evening of the same day. Dāvid looked tired and drawn as he greeted me in the court-yard of the convent. He was inordinately pleased to see me. He kissed my hand so beautifully.

I was glad I had come promptly to support him through the funeral. It was quite an ordeal even for me with no particular links, an extremely mournful occasion with horses, black plumes and the pomp and ceremony Roman Catholics demanded for a much respected benefactor well known in the community. It seemed the whole of San d'Almazzo village and much of Florence turned out for the event as well as representatives of hospitals throughout the land.

The Signora did not attend but continued to make faces behind her window.

"I wish the Blessed Virgin would take her away," expressed a frowning Dāvid, "I cannot bear to see her making those faces."

"They say she is quite happy."

"She would be happier dead," he groaned.

We took Mass together side by side at the funeral.

It reminded me of when Gough and I had taken Communion in the Great Oaks chapel.

Dāvid's and my relationship was wonderfully companionable. Whether it was just sitting on the terraces together not saying much, or my reading to him the old classics from the convent library, or going for walks, or my watching him paint with his left hand, it was the same. We enjoyed being together, and that was not all. We loved to touch. I liked to take his arm, to hold his hand, to feel when out walking his great height beside me. We always kissed good-night. There was no truck with Dāvid who liked to kiss me on the lips!

One day on the terraces when I was so happy to be with him and was dreading the thought of having to go back soon and pick up my life in England again (how I would miss the sun, the companionship) Dāvid said with a wry smile, "I would like to go down on my knees to my beautiful English Princess, but that might be disastrous! I would most probably topple over, so I will sit here and hold your hand in mine like this and ask you if you will marry an old wounded war horse who knows not who he is or where he came from, and make me the happiest man in Italy. I was miserable when you left. I love being with you. I love you very much, Isabella. What do you say?"

"I can only say 'Si', Dāvid, for I love you too!"

And so it was arranged. We were married in the little chapel in the convent by the interior glassed-in courtyard where the Signora sat making faces from her window. All the nuns came beaming their sweet smiles beneath their blue coiffs for the joy of a romance under their ancient roof, and for seeing the Signor Dāvid, whose life they had saved, so happy.

There were many things that had to be done before we could go on honeymoon to England to meet the boys and show Dāvid all the things he wanted to see. There were documents to sign and lawyers to visit, for old Signor Landi had had left his *casa* and the bulk of his money to Dāvid with a proviso for the Signora to be looked after by the nuns for the rest of her life, until, by the grace of God, she would join him, which time, Dāvid fervently hoped, would be soon.

The tenants at the *casa* had to be given notice so that Dāvid and I could live there and he could have his studio again. Yes, there was a great deal to be accomplished and Dāvid found he could do far more with his 'lazy' mind than he had at one time thought. He also found, when I encouraged him to take modern occupational therapy, that his wasted muscles improved. And especially he enjoyed swimming. He loved the water, he said. It never ceased to amaze me – all the similarities . . .

Another thing. Dāvid had taken on the British expletive of 'bloody', goodness knows where from. I hardly ever used it not being given to swearing. I had never heard old Signor Landi use it, and the nuns certainly did not! The word burst forth in exasperated moments when he tripped over something, or crashed one of Sister Mary's tea cups. "Look at what my bloody arm – or hand, or leg – has caused me to do," made me laugh. Although it genuinely amused me to hear him use the word, I also laughed to make light of the incident, show him there was no need to be so upset or let the accident depress him. He would

246

look at me seriously cross with himself and then smile. "I like to see you laugh," he would say, "you have such pretty teeth Isabella. If my clumsiness makes you happy, *é bené*, it is worth it!"

Dāvid positively sparkled in England when we went on our honeymoon. It was all new to him. And I saw it again through him. He loved the green fields, and he loved Scotland too where he sketched the moors and the purple heather. We stayed with Babs' son in the 'Keep' his parents had repaired. The spiral stone stairs, with a loose rope for bannister, were a nightmare for Dāvid and for me as he hated to be helped. I was glad to move him on all in one piece. And of course he met my sons and their families.

Most of all on that first visit to Great Britain, Dāvid enjoyed the Dorset countryside where he liked to follow in Gough's footsteps to vicariously fill-in his lost past. We visited Winchester College and saw Gough's name inscribed on the 'In Memoriam' panel. We went to Great Oaks Hall, by now a permanent boarding school. We visited the little chapel in the grounds and laid flowers on Geoffrey, Adele and Benjamin's grave; and we went to Bovington to see the tanks on Open Day. We faced the sea in a stiff breeze at Lulworth Cove, took a boat across Poole harbour, and did many more of the things I had done before.

"Now you have seen where Gough lived as a child, where he grew up, and where he drove his tank through the quiet villages of Dorset," I said in the aeroplane on our way home, home to the Landis' *casa* of beautiful views.

"*Si*, my beloved Isabella. Now I can picture where

247

you walked with Gough. I have taken on the cloak of that man in the black beret you loved so much. In this way I too have a past. In this way I have grown from babyhood and boyhood to when I was a man and can remember."

Several times a year my sons with their wives and children come out to visit us. We have built a swimming pool on one of the terraces for their enjoyment, though mainly for Dāvid to exercise in it daily. You cannot imagine how much he has improved from the slow-moving man I first saw in the convent. He has also undergone reconstruction on his head, ear, and face. During these operations I stayed in my younger son's home where John's parents used to live, near to Cambridge and its specialized hospital of plastic surgery. On marriage I had sold my stable block to friends of Dulcie.

For the recuperation period we went to Gough's son. He lives in Matravers country. John and I had told him early on that he was a Nicholson. He is very proud of his father's record, and when grown up gravitated to Dorset quite naturally, drawn by ties deep down in his roots.

One of my great pleasures is to see my grandchildren playing with Dāvid whom they call 'Nonno', the Italian familiar for 'Grandpa'. They love him dearly. The younger ones are fascinated by his wounds which are, since they were 'tidied up', not so terrible as they once were though he still wears the beret not only to hide the scars but because, as he says, tanks brought us together. He declares the badge is more precious than any jewel could be. Occasionally he allows the children to peep under the beret and see the scarring which they view with awe and horrified delight. The expression on their faces instead of causing him to cringe and want to hide, makes him tease them further with tall tales of desert battles he has read about in history books.

"Two men in black berets have I loved in my life," I whisper cosy in bed in Dāvid's arms after our lovemaking when the house is very quiet and the children have all gone, "but it is *this* man that I love now, and only he."

"Ah, *mia bella* of the beautiful name, how happy you make me," Dāvid sighs contentedly. "Our life together is the miracle."

Since the intimacies of my marriage bed, there are things I secretly treasure in my heart and will not reveal.

I have no need to search more for long buried evidence. All that matters now is that Dāvid and I found each other and love one another. Indeed we fell in love at first sight when I rose from my chaise-longue on the garden path to make room to let him pass. The magic was there – *is* there.

'*Ritornello*'. Dulcie said it. Ah yes, *ritornello* indeed.

I am back in love again . . .